Jungle Dog Justice

To all the Souls that never made it home
from foreign soil

I

Scott Finlay woke up in a feverish sweat. Salt crystals had formed a crust on his lower back from the profuse sweating and evaporation. It was beginning to make him itchy. The room he was in felt like being outside in a fog. The supersaturated air was so heavy, a pocket knife would cut a slice you could swallow. He started to get dizzy and the nausea crept up from deep in his stomach. The bile-infused saliva was dripping from the tip of his cotton-mouthed tongue. Scott was brain-fogged and unsure of where, exactly, he was. He was feeling much like the morning after a drinking blitz and blackout. He started the hangover tradition of trying to recall, moment by moment, everything he could remember doing from the time he woke up yesterday at 7 o'clock: breakfast, a quick shower, getting dressed...then it all starts getting hazy. He remembered being in one of the local bars in Federal Hill, Baltimore that evening. He was fighting to understand the room he woke up in... He didn't recognize any of it; not a single piece of the furnishings. Scott had gotten drunk like this hundreds of times before and always woke up back in his room, in his studio apartment overlooking the park in Locust Point. He reached up to rub his eyes and a surge of pain and panic overcame him. He immediately passed out.

What seemed like hours later, Scott woke to an even more pressing pain. His hands were throbbing in rhythm with his heartbeat. He reached up to wipe the saliva that was dripping off his chin and a pain shot through his hand like it was stuck in an electrical socket. The impulses grew to an intensity that wouldn't allow his brain to work. It was overriding anything else he could think about. Instinctually, he glanced down at his hands and noticed they were wrapped in gauze bandages, with small dots of blood. This shock, coupled with the intense electrical pains he was feeling, caused the vessels in his brain to spasm and he immediately fainted again.

When he finally woke from the second fainting spell, in the most intense pain, he tried to move and sat up on the unfamiliar bed. In a panic, he started searching for a source of better light. The current ambient light in the room was just enough to establish the depth perception he needed to see the bed in relation to the floor. He dropped his arms to push off and stand up, when he did another surge of intense pain, radiating this time from both his hands, reached all the way to the roots of his teeth. They began to chatter uncontrollably and he, again, panicked. His fight or flight response caused an immediate dump of adrenaline into his bloodstream and his heart felt like it was going to jump out and start beating him, rhythmically, in the head. The ringing in his ears got so intense that he couldn't even hear the swishing of the sheets or his footfalls on the floor as he ambled around the room in search of a lamp or light switch.

He noticed a faint beam of light coming from the gap in the bottom of the door and he went over to it. As he reached for the doorknob, the bandages interfered with his ability to grip the handle and open it. He knelt down to try and peak through the gap in the door. The pain intensified now to a roar and his every thought was consumed with the thumping of his heart, which was in perfect timing with the pains in his hands. As soon as he placed them on the floor to help him balance, he was out again...

Scott Finlay was a contractor by trade. He never really cared to learn anything else in his life. At 35, he thought this was as good as it got. He had steady work in the neighborhoods around the city. He had a roof over his head in a neighborhood that he was familiar with and was familiar with him. He chose the life he was leading and seemed content with it for the most part.

He spent his disposable income betting on sports and drinking in the local bars. Saving money was never a priority. This was the case for most of his close friends because they all lived at home with their parents and didn't have any bills. None of them had more than a high school education and weren't looking to go anywhere more than right there in that small South Baltimore neighborhood between Federal Hill to the West and Ft McHenry to the East.

The small community was mostly made up of longshoreman, 2nd and 3rd generation immigrant transplants, and people that worked in the small factories that tickled the area. A plastic cup factory on Fort Avenue, Domino Sugar down the Point, and the old McCormicks spice company were the main employers for the area. Small shipyards dotted the shorelines between the harbor and the bay as well as several marine port terminals. It could be said that South Baltimore was generally made up of white, blue collar, middle class Americans that were incredibly proud of where and who they were. Mostly Roman Catholic, immigrant families from the British isles, Germany and Poland. They had a strong work ethic and liked to play even harder on their time off. There was a bar or small restaurant on almost every street, each with its own set of loyal patrons. This was the way that Scott grew up and where he got his moral code.

He finally woke up after what felt like another day. There was no reference for him to establish whether it was the morning or evening and the several times that he passed out and woke back up weren't helping. He was still on the floor, next to the door with the light coming in from the bottom gap. He heard voices outside the door and started to yell for help. He was kicking the door with his feet and holding his arms above his head, which helped with the intense thumping pain that seemed to follow every beat of his quick paced heart.

Finally, a voice from the other side of the door asked who was in there. It was a woman's voice. He begged her to open the door and to his amazement, the door was unlocked. As he looked out from the floor, he saw the light was from a hallway that led to a couple of other doors. As soon as the young lady took one look at Scott she screeched like a wounded hawk and ran down the hall. Scott called out for her to stop and help but his appearance and the bloody bandaged hands were enough to make her run for her life.

Scott managed to roll over and elbow his way up on his feet using the wall. He followed after her and went out an open door leading to the street. The sun was blinding as he tried to gain some clue to where he was. The sweet, metallic smell of blood was thick in the air and the train tracks leading to the building next door made him think of only one place...Pigtown. He figured that the building was the old slaughterhouse because of the noise and stench. One of the neighborhood lowlifes ran over and tried to bum a twenty for his crack habit.

As he stood there smiling through his glass pipe smoking, brown-tinged teeth, Scott begged him for help. He would give him whatever he wanted if he did. The guy was so high he just kept smiling while helping Scott remove the bandage on his left arm. When he saw the carnage that was once his hands, that he used for his livelihood, he immediately let out a primal scream. The squealing of the pigs in the slaughterhouse caught up with the noise and he could be heard throughout the entire neighborhood for blocks. Scott was missing all of his fingers, including his thumbs. All he was able to make out were the backs and palms of his hands. They were swollen, purple and black from the trauma of having his fingers removed. The last thing he remembered after that view was the fast approaching pavement as his face struck the sidewalk with a thud. Lights out and good night. No pain, no suffering, just horror, pure, unadulterated horror!...

Mr. Finlay arrived in this terrifying predicament because he was a pedophile. He liked to abuse children and most importantly, he liked to diddle little girls. He was always attracted to younger girls and the trauma that led to his behavior as an adult started when he was about 8. He had some neighborhood girls, about the same age, that were always hanging about and wanting to play. At that age, hormones beginning to blossom, playing doctor was one of many ways to enjoy the company of others.

He had one of those old Fisher Price doctor sets. The one with the foam-based stethoscope and fat plastic thermometer that had a slider to indicate the temperature. Those girls were ahead of their time and little Scott was loving it. He would get them to take off their clothes and lay on the couch in his basement so he could "examine" them. He liked to see their naked bodies and compare them to his. They reminded him of little conch shells he saw in the books on his parent's shelves. He liked to use the plastic thermometer, that was included in the doctors kit, to slide around between their legs. They didn't seem to mind. As a matter of fact, they would all giggle about it while they were laying there.

One day, while he was performing his "examination" on the girl across the street, her mother came over to fetch her for dinner. When Scott's mother called down the basement and didn't get a response, both parents went down to see what was going on. With the music from the phonograph blaring a loud Bruce Hornsby's " The Way it Is," the two didn't notice their parents coming down the stairs. His mother let out a yelp while the girl's mother grabbed her daughter to separate the two. Scott was totally naked, standing there with the plastic thermometer in his hand while his friend started to cry and hide herself in shame. The girl's mother, in a rage, ran up the stairs with her daughter, shouting threats of litigation.

Mortified at what she just witnessed, Scott's mom started beating him unmercifully, eventually sending him to his room for the rest of the night without any supper. She added the threat of waiting until his father got home to hear what he had done. No terror could strike at the heart of a school-aged child more than the threat of waiting until your father got home from work. Once his father heard about this incident, all hell was going to reign down on Scott. He started to shake and cry uncontrollably. He was daydreaming the ways he was going to be punished; up to and including a beating that could possibly kill him. His father was particularly good with the belt. He liked to fold it in half and flail his son like Jesus before the cross. Being young and impressionable, the terror and beatings contributed to his behavior when he became an adult.

During his pubescent years he thought of those young girls often and it drove him absolutely crazy. In early adulthood he knew, deep inside, how sick it was to be thinking about fondling them like that but he couldn't help himself. His dark thoughts followed him around everywhere and in everything he did. He was obsessed with them. The sad part about all of it was the damage he passed on from his soul to all those young girls that he was sexually abusing.

He would find girls in the park or at the mall. One of his favorite spots was the playground in the adjacent neighborhood where he would stalk his next prey. He treated it just like he was hunting a deer. He was patient and used the occasional piece of candy or a sweet as bait. He lured his young victims into his car and would talk them into removing whatever pants or dress they were wearing. Then he would begin to stroke the girl with his fingers. Without fully inserting them, he would rub in between their legs while he manipulated himself. Most of the girls were in such a state of shock at the touching that they rarely put up a fight for fear of retribution.

The shame they feel is so real and strong that the idea of telling their parents is completely out of the question. This is the real tragedy. They are so traumatized by these events that they are scared to tell anyone. Scared for fear of disbelief, blame, insults, and hurt they may endure by confiding in someone. Imagine living with this affliction and trying to have a normal, healthy relationship with a family and kids of your own. What Scott was doing was not just affecting these girls in the now but for the rest of their born days on this earth. For some it is so emotionally shattering that they wind up, years later, committing suicide because they aren't able to cope. Scott was an abuser and a potential murderer by effect.

He eventually woke up with a hoard of people standing around him, asking each other if he was dead. They all leered at him with the typical crackhead, toothless smile and disheveled hair that hadn't been washed in a week. The pavement face plant caused an enormous hematoma to form on his forehead. He had some chips of something along with blood in his mouth. After probing around with his tongue, he realized that the chips came from his front teeth. His bottom lip was bleeding from cuts made by the broken teeth. He managed to speak to someone in the crowd and asked for help getting up. One of them shouted something about the blood stain on the back of his shirt and as they were helping him stand up, another one lifted his shirt, exposing an angry red and black looking splotch right smack in the middle of his back. It was hard to make out but appeared to be about the size of a softball. It was shaped like a shield. There was a dog in the middle with a lightening bolt and some sort of cross behind it. Also visible were the numbers 2 and 1. No one was sober enough to figure it out but they all shouted at Scott that he needed to get to the hospital to take care of the two stumps he had where his fingers used to be.

II

Two weeks in the stifling jungles of Colombia is enough to drive a person mad. It was Garrett's last overseas assignment before being discharged and going home. The streets of Baltimore were a lot different from where he was now. Endless hours sitting in a tarp covered hole in the ground, which served as an observation post. His unit used these posts to gain intelligence on the drug operations of the many lords that ruled this area of the world. Garrett was a member of one of the darkest and most unknown units in all of special operations, the Jungle Dogs. The one and only purpose of this group was to gather intelligence and dismantle cocaine processing labs by any means necessary. The targets were scattered over 762,000 square km from the Colombian Andean National Region to the Amazonian Basin in the South. Most of this terrain, approximately 60% of the country, is extremely difficult and only accessible by foot, boat, and pack animal.

Garrett was an intelligent man and breezed through his academic years with the ease of a figure skater on the ice. He was 30 when the army recruited him into the group and he had already served 2 tours in South and Central America. He was a medical sergeant with the 7th Special Forces Group in Florida. The Green Beret had always been his ultimate prize and when he received it, none of his family was there to celebrate with him. He didn't have any family to speak of.

He was terribly introverted and most of the guys in his company thought there was something wrong with him. He rarely spoke unless treating someone that was wounded in the multitude of combat operations he participated in. One thing that Garrett had going for him throughout his deployments was repetition. Sometimes the drone of doing the same types of things day in and day out help to break the monotony of missions like the one he was on today. Sitting in a hootch in the middle of the jungle heat isn't for everyone.

His training taught him that the mission was always critical and achieving it was the only thing that mattered. Whatever needed to be done, was to be done. No questions asked; no bitching, no moaning, just complete the mission and make it back to base. He wasn't sure how he felt to finally be going home. He imagined a lifetime of experiences were condensed into his deployments. He had no idea that life had a way of continuing on with or without you.

Scrolling through the Baltimore Sun one spring afternoon, Garrett came across an article in the police blotter about a man that was arrested for sexual assault of a minor. This scumbag had a rap sheet the proverbial *mile long*. He was a felon with at least 12 charges in several states as well as several misdemeanor battery charges. Armed robbery and auto theft were also on there. This was a real waste product of life. An oxygen thief, as Garrett liked to say... This guy was the amoeba that lived on the shit that came out of the foulest creatures on the planet. A real danger to society. It occurred to Garrett that the judicial system had failed the public miserably. *Why was he still out walking around? And caught in the most heinous crime of them all, sexual assault on a child*, Garrett proselytized. According to him it was way worse then murdering someone. It ravaged the soul of the victim. This tore out whatever little bit of humanity there was within a person. Then stomped on it, shit and spit on it, and then sent it back inside to fester for the rest of that person's life. It was abhorrent, it was just down right evil.

Garrett wasn't a religious person, although he was raised in the church, but he cared very much about what was right and wrong. It was after reading about this arrest that he felt like he finally found a purpose in his civilian life. The time during the drug wars, running around in the jungles of Colombia and burning, killing, and generally reaping the worst kind of havoc on local villages really did a number on Garrett. He was not the same person after all that. And the worst part about it was that he never got any recognition because it was all top secret.

His team infiltrated mountainous, jungle country and disappeared for months at a time working off the bits and pieces of intelligence they collected. Most of the labs were set up outside small villages and the work being done involved processing coco paste into cocaine hydrochloride. It was a multi-step process involving the addition of different chemicals to the paste, forming different precipitates. These are then filtered and dried with fans or lamps to the crystalline powder that is the final product. The cocaine made its way from South America to the shores of Miami. The smugglers even used their profits to build small submersibles that could go unnoticed through the bay waters off the coast and be delivered to waiting vessels under the cover of darkness.

Garrett spent the next couple of weeks obsessing about this guy that had the audacity to hurt a young child in that way. He spent hours trying to decipher the type of mind it would take to do this. During his life, he had crossed people that had sociopathic and schizophrenic tendencies and just couldn't understand how that could turn into an assault on a little girl's innocence. Garrett didn't have any kids himself. He cringed at the thought of any child having to go through that kind of mental torture for the rest of their lives. He read somewhere about the probabilities of increased risk in suicide from traumas like this later in life. The child turns into an adult and can't shake the unwarranted shame and guilt they feel about things that happened to them years earlier. He couldn't picture a child or adult having to live with that hanging over their heads.

He started to formulate a plan to ensure that something like that would never happen from this putrid shit stain again. He searched in the public records to find out everything he could about this monster. It was the first time he decided this wasn't a person at all.

It was a creature, an evil monster like the ones that you fear are living under your bed or in your closet when you are a child. It was unbearable and he was starting to get crushing sinus headaches whenever he thought too hard about these things. He could feel his skin crawl and even caught himself shaking uncontrollably when he found out that the man was released, again, on a bond, allowed back into society. No house arrest, no monitoring, just free in the Baltimore area to create more destruction and ruin more lives. He got so angry, he started wondering about the presiding judge on the case, trying to figure out how he missed this multiple offenders past. He felt like the judge was a bit responsible for allowing this mutant to roam his once beautiful streets in search of another victim or victims to harm in whatever foul way his sick brain would allow.

Traveling from one government building to another, he was able to get an address for this scumbag. It turned out that he was close, in the Locust Point area of town, not far from where he lived. This just added fuel to his already angry fire because he could picture all of the neighborhood kids that he knew suffering under the hands of this deranged and obviously vicious creature. *A succubus!* That was the word he was looking for. *No, a succubus is a female witch that seduces men. What is a soul sucking, energy sapping deviant? Got it! A fucking vampire...Nosferatu himself. An emotional vampire.* That was exactly what this unearthly creature was to Garrett. He just couldn't get enough of thinking about ways to make this guy suffer. And then it dawned on him. Death was too good for this piece of shit! This mother fucker was going to live the rest of his life in complete awareness of his crimes against humanity. He was going to have to spend the rest of his born days in constant reflection. But how could he provide this service that he so greatly wanted to bestow?

"Ill cut off his fucking fingers!" he exclaimed out loud while walking down Fort Ave. People were looking at him, obviously not understanding because what they heard was so out of context. People were looking at him to see if he was wearing earbuds and wondering who he was talking to. Was he addressing someone on the street? People were passing him as he walked and thinking he must be one of the crazy homeless people from downtown screeching and blurting out things to no-one in particular.

"That is exactly what I'll do to this monster. I'll cut off every fucking one of his fingers and let him live with the idea that someone else will have to take care of him and wipe his filthy ass for the rest of his time on this earth!" Garrett was, by nature, an obsessive and sometimes compulsive person. It is what helped him get through all the years of training to become a Green Beret. All of the different schools and field exercises, where solid knowledge of your strengths and weaknesses, were somewhat easy for him because of his self awareness. His obsessions concerning this man, he was abhorred at the idea of even calling him a man, were turning into a laser guided and focused beam very much like the laser designator he used to tag targets for bombing runs.

Garrett spent the next couple of weeks scoping out different places where he could inflict his painful plan. He also staked out the address he found for the monster. When he finally found the shithead, he was astounded at the way he was so freely walking around without a care in the world. He wanted to walk across the park, drag him in the alley, and really work on him before slitting his throat. One cannot imagine the self control he invoked to ensure that he stuck to the plan.

He spent a lot of evenings figuring out the details to restrain and remove all of the digits on his hands. He came to the conclusion that his best recourse for both security and plan success was to anesthetize the punk first, then using a pair of lopping shears, he would remove all the fingers. He also came up with the idea of marking him or more specifically, branding him with an iron like you would to a cow that belonged on your ranch. The lopping shears he could procure at just about any lawn and garden center. Using cash, so as not to be traced, he would purchase the shears and some duct tape to secure the arms to a chair. The problem he was having was figuring out what to use for the anesthesia. Where could he get something that would buy him time to perform the procedure? After a bit of digging, he decided on the old school approach with either ether or chloroform, both of which are readily available online through lab supply companies. He could purchase it with a fake account using a prepaid credit card. Being a medic, he was sure he could figure out all the detailed procedures for its use. Now that he had the basic idea of what to do, he just needed to work the plan out in practice a few times.

He would integrate it into a master plan after he surveilled this guy's schedule and found a hole to use for a "grab and go". It was going to be a tight run but he had the experience of being a special operator and had done lots of this type of thing while he was serving in South America. It was not uncommon for his team to infiltrate, through complete silence, a lab and take out all the security first. He was well versed in the silent killing techniques using both a suppressed weapon as well as his tactical knife. He actually prided himself on his ability to be a silent killer in those scenarios. It is a real art to be able to sneak up on a patrol guard from behind when most of their senses are honed and heightened while on duty. It is their one and only job to ensure a safe and secure site for the workers. Garrett was sure that he was going to have no problem drugging and grabbing the monster.

The next phase was the transportation, to a yet undiscovered place, to perform the amputations. He had searched around a lot of the lower neighborhoods of Baltimore and decided that across the train tracks to the East was his best option. He knew of a loft type housing project that was abandoned after the financial downturn. It was being built near the slaughterhouse in Pigtown. This neighborhood was one of the more drug infested haunts that surrounded the city. It was predominately a poor, white neighborhood with row homes and small businesses that surrounded and supported the slaughterhouse and its employees. The train brought the pigs from surrounding farms in the exterior counties and unloaded them for an approximately 500 meter march down the road, which is how the neighborhood got its name. The pigs are slaughtered and then taken via truck to wholesalers in the city. From there, the pork is sent throughout the country and distributed to the retail markets. Garrett liked the idea of using this neighborhood because the attention was normally drawn to the slaughterhouse. Most of the inhabitants are so whacked out during the day that bringing in his work will pretty much go unnoticed. The close proximity to the slaughterhouse and noise from the pigs will mask any that he might make during his operation.

He made his way into the abandoned warehouse, where there were loft style apartments in various stages of completion. Of course, all the valuable appliances and copper had long been removed by the neighborhood vandals and sold for scrap at one of the myriad yards throughout the city. He decided on a nice ground entrance apartment at the end of one of the halls that already had a chair, a small table, and a twin mattress lying on a wooden frame. Perhaps it was the haunt of some homeless person but looked like it hadn't been lived in for a while. Garrett brought in a battery operated lantern for light and started to prep the room for the execution phase of his operation. Garrett had an acquaintance that worked in a machine tool shop in Curtis Bay. He took one of his unit patches to his friend and asked him to make a metal brand with a two foot handle. He told him it was for some woodworking projects and this would help him mark them with a personal logo. He knew he had to come up with some story and that was the best he could think of at the time.

His unit patch was a shield-shaped outline with a two-toned background of green and white. Directly in the center of the shield was a bust of a black/grey, short-eared dog. It was looking to the right of the shield. Behind the dog were a crossed dagger and yellow lightening bolt contrasting the green and white background. On the outer edges of the shield, adjacent to the dog's bust were the numbers 2 on the left and 1 on the right. This was his unit's radio call numbers. He was proud of this symbol and thought it would make a great brand that his unit could use to induct new members. Turns out that he had a much darker use for it and he felt it would be a way to mark his work on this shithead. He would brand It as if he owned It for the rest of Its miserable life. He wasn't worried too much about anyone recognizing the brand because of the clandestine nature of his outfit and the obscurity of his unit even within the special operations command. In fact, his unit was so secretive that congress only saw the line items of expenses through a slush fund that was set up by the pentagon at the highest levels. Just another layer of darkness, cloaked in nothingness other than a handful of men that were willing to risk their lives for one of the worst scourges to ever hit the United States.

While his friend was working on the brand and he was waiting for the chloroform to arrive at a shady PO Box that he rented for a month in a fictitious name. He paid for it with a prepaid visa that he got at the local CVS. His next barrier to overcome was a vehicle he could use to transport this fuckface. He figured a van would be best but he wasn't sure if he should boost one or rent one. The idea of renting one seemed obvious but the process allowed for an unwanted paper trail. He we going to steal one from a neighborhood far from any of the action.

The next day he found the perfect van, a late 80s Volkswagen that he found all the way around the beltway in Dundalk. It had been parked in a lot for a few days and looked like it had been there for quite a while. He marked the tires, like a parking officer would, with chalk and came back the next day to see if it had moved. His luck had it still there in the same place, unmoved. It was in an older lot that was for the drive-in theatre. It was well positioned and away from any of the houses nearby. He felt that he could steal it during the evening when there was little if any light and either ditch it or bring it right back without anyone taking notice. In his youth, in South Baltimore, his questionable neighborhood friends had stolen several cars. He would watch how they did it and kept that with him into his adulthood. His youth wasn't always colored in roses. He had his share of rebelling as most teenagers do, drinking, smoking weed, and generally being a nuisance. His father worked in Federal Hill at the old General Electric Plant and his mother was a homemaker/neighborhood gossip. She spent most of her days over at the neighbors playing cards and drinking homemade wine. He had the run of the neighborhood after school with his friends and during the entire summer.

When his plan started to take its final form, Garrett was getting that same feeling inside that he got before he was deployed into the jungle. He usually couldn't sleep very well a week before, which he remedied with booze and Benadryl. He also got that low down in the stomach sick feeling that people get when you have to give a speech in front of a crowd of people. He was beginning to feel these symptoms and his training kicked in. It was time to focus and make sure he had details and contingencies.

He had a van for the transportation phase. He made sure there was plenty of room in the back and was able to start the vehicle. He did a dress rehearsal for the theft but didn't take the van anywhere. He took his homemade slimjim, which was just a flat piece of sheet metal he found on trash day in someones bin. By adding a notch to one of the ends, he could hook the lever that opened the door. He made sure there was no alarm. It was a late 80's model, sitting in an empty lot, so he felt confident about that. It really was pure luck that he happened to find this perfect van in such a place…it was almost like it was meant to be. After he popped the door and did a quick inspection of the inside, he popped the plastic cowling that covered the steering column and loosened all the wires. He traced and found the battery and starter wires and stripped them. He gave them a quick touch and to his surprise, they sparked and he felt the solenoid kick in to turn the flywheel. So the battery was good, and he had the correct wires.

Now he wanted to make sure there was fuel and for this he just put a stick down the fill spout and it came back with what appeared to be about half a tank. It was getting light out so he decided to just give it a quick try and see if it would fully engage and run the engine. With the simple touching of the wires and a quick twist, the motor was humming along like it never had any problems. The van was not automatic but had a manual stick shift on the floor between the two front seats. It had been a minute since he operated a manual transmission but he looked at it like riding a bike…it would turn into muscle memory and he would figure it out. He untwisted the wires, which turned the engine off. He delicately placed the cowling back on the steering column, locked the door, and went to his car that he parked a couple of blocks away. Van: check!

The chloroform that he ordered arrived a couple of days later and he turned in the keys to the post box so that he wouldn't be associated with it anymore. He traveled all the way across town to get that box in the North end of the city near MLK Boulevard. It was in a shady neighborhood and he was sure he wouldn't be recognized because most of that part of the hood were black, lower class people that served in the hospitality industries downtown. Anesthetic: check!

He spent a day at the abandoned apartment trying to arrange the things in there so that there was a good flow from the door to the chair, and then to the mattress. As for a pillow, he found an old gym bag filled with a bunch of used, stinky clothes and he thought that was befitting the scumbag that would be using it. The final details were starting to come together so he took a trip to the nearest garden center at the Walmart and purchased a cheap pair of very sharp lopping shears. When he got home he went to the neighbors yard and tried them out on thumb sized branches on the bushes in her backyard. It cut through them as if they weren't even there. These were going to work perfect to cleanly sever the digits of the dirtbag's hands. He considered shearing off his penis as well but opted against it because of the risk of significant blood loss it might cause. Garrett wasn't trying to kill It. That was not the original vision. This thought made him realize he was going to need to cauterize the stubs or this thing could possibly bleed to death. After removing them all there would possibly be a vast amount of arterial blood loss. The only other option was to use a couple genII tourniquets at his wrists. He opted to use a plumbing torch to both heat the brand that he was going to use as well as fuse the bloody ends of the removed digits. Blood-loss mitigation: check!

The final details were in the bandaging that he would put over the stumps to help stave off any ancillary blood loss as well as mask the original fright so that this guy had time to think about his situation. Garrett finalized everything on Monday and decided he would make his move on Wednesday. He knew where he lived, how he traveled, which was so pitifully predictable, and he knew what he would most likely be doing on that evening until about 2am the next day. Wednesdays were Busch League Billiards night at the Southside Saloon on Fort Avenue in Federal Hill and Scott was a member of the team. He would be drinking and playing pool until closing time and then stumble down the hill to Locust Point and his miserable apartment on the second floor of a row home near the park. Garrett had his plan and he was sticking to it.

III

Wednesday, 2230p, Dundalk. Two blocks from the empty lot at the abandoned drive-in.

Garrett was sitting in his car waiting for the perfect moment to walk to the drive-in lot and boost the Volkswagen van. His nerves were starting to get the better of him and he took a slug off the bottle of Johnnie Walker Red that he had in the seat next to him. He was partial to the Red because that is what he drank with his friends in high school. It was usually that or Wild Turkey, depending what was in his parents liquor cabinet, but the Turkey never settled well in Garrett's stomach like the good ole Red. His parents served the Turkey to guests and saved the smooth Johnnie Walker for themselves. After about two slugs of liquid courage, he noticed that he felt a moment of complete calm. He opened the back door and grabbed his day bag out of the back seat. Inside was the chloroform, a rag, the custom brand, garden loppers, plumber's torch, and bandages he would need for the rest of the operation. He went ahead and stuck the bottle of Red in the bag as well and headed down the street towards the drive-in.

He passed a few people walking their dogs but for the most part the neighborhood was deserted. It was a school night and everyone was settling down for the evening. He couldn't help but be a little apprehensive about the van and prayed that everything would go smoothly. He thought about a breathing technique he learned in the service to calm the mind and body before the action. He had used this technique thousands of times in the field when in enemy territory and found it helpful during times of personal crisis now that he was out. Imagining a square, while breathing in to the count of

4, start visualizing a dot moving along the top line in a clockwise direction. When 4 is reached at the corner, start exhaling as the dot traces the right hand line to the bottom of the square. Again, when the bottom right corner is reached at the count of 4, begin inhaling again as the dot traces the bottom line towards the left. Finally, upon reaching the bottom left corner the last count of four is an exhalation until the dot reaches the top left corner. After he did this, he noticed that his mind was completely calm. He wasn't thinking about the risks involved with boosting the van. He was also starting to feel the two swigs he took of the Red.

He took out his homemade slimjim and opened the driver's door. Continuing seamlessly, he removed the steering column's cowling and searched for the wires that he previously stripped. He touched them together, got a spark and knew that the battery was still good. He reached over to the passenger seat and grabbed the bottle of Red and took one more large swallow. It burnt so bad and entered his nasal cavity. He couldn't help but let out a horrible cough and his eyes began to water. He decided that was enough and put the wires together with a twist.

The van started and to Garrett's surprise, the radio was blaring loud on some country station! It scared the living shit out of him and he immediately, instinctively, ducked down into the space under the steering wheel. It was reactionary, he had been in so many fire fights that his initial instinct was to find cover and then return fire. A momentary glimpse into his soul revealed a scared kid that hated loud noises. The radio was only a trigger for his training. All operators eventually process the sound of a weapon. It doesn't matter if it is a handgun or a rifle. The initial instinct is to run and hide. Operators are desensitized to the sounds and learn to take cover. Running is not an option. Hide or drop, check your weapon for action and ammunition, evaluate the situation, and engage the threat. All of this happens in a couple of seconds. Garrett was so tuned to this, that he didn't realize that the "threat" was just a car radio.

With a beating heart and shaking hands, He turned the radio off and started to do a few seconds of the breathing exercise again. It was a minute or two before he undid the emergency brake and put the gear in first. Garret hadn't driven a manual transmission since his childhood. With an obligatory shutter, the van took off towards the center of the lot. Garrett steered the van in a wide circle to do quick check before giving it some gas and heading towards the beltway back to Federal Hill. He decided that taking the route through the city, Boston Street through Fells Point, was the best chance of avoiding any unnecessary police and CCTV cameras that would surely be observing the tunnels to the other side of the Bay. It was either that or the Key Bridge and he wasn't in the mood for the scenic route. One final check of the van, the gas was at the halfway mark, the day pack was in the backseat, so he was off to good start...

At 2230 on a weeknight in Baltimore, there isn't a lot of traffic to contend with so he arrived at the Fed Hill neighborhood in about 20 minutes. He decided to go straight to the Point and find a place to park the van for a good surveillance vantage while he waited for his prey to arrive. *Dammit!* He forgot to grab some snacks. All the movies he watched about stakeouts involved snacks and lots of coffee. Garrett was not a coffee drinker and it was too late to go to Ms. Moon's convenience store on the next corner for chips.

He waited patiently in the van adjacent to the park in one of the alley streets. He figured that his only risk at this point would be one of the police cruisers spotting him blocking the alley and approaching him for questioning. Other than that, everyone else was either in one of the corner bars getting blitzed or home sleeping for work tomorrow. Being a school night and late, all of the neighborhood kids were either home, watching TV, or in bed.

Latrobe Park looked like a ghost town. It wasn't long ago that they redid the multi-use field and installed astroturf. That fake grass that is popular in professional football stadiums. He actually shivered a little thinking about the pain a face plant into it going about 15 miles an hour must feel. *That has to hurt*, he thought. *Well, wait until I get a hold of this fucking Scott! He doesn't know what pain is. What I'm gonna do to him is gonna give him a lifetime of pain, physical and mental. If he decides to leave the world because of it, that's on him...I don't want to be responsible for his death, just his constant suffering.*

After what seemed like hours, Garrett looked at his watch and realized that it was almost go time. In the rearview mirror, he saw Scott coming down the street. Stumbling and leaning along the walls of the row homes to help him keep upright. He was about a block away, so Garrett reached over to his bag and grabbed the rag and bottle of chloroform. After saturating the rag and gagging a bit, he placed both in his jacket pocket and left the van. He went around to the back of the van and opened one of the doors just enough so that he wouldn't have to fiddle with it when he arrived with Scott. He positioned himself for the strike and took out the chloroform soaked rag. As soon as he came around the corner and turned towards the back door to the building, Garrett struck.

From a vantage point behind Scott, he grabbed his right, dominant arm by the wrist and at the same time put the anesthetic saturated rag over his nose and mouth. There really wasn't much of a struggle, Scott was already inebriated to the point of incapacitation. All Garrett did was catch him as he fell back, supporting him under both armpits. He put the rag back in his pocket and arranged him so that one of Scott's arms was around his shoulder, as if he was supporting a drunk friend and trying to help him home. He walked rather clumsily to the back of the van, which was no more than 10 feet away and kicked open the back door with his foot. Without a lot of care, he threw Scott into the back of the van, grabbed both his shoes, which were still hanging out the back, and shoved him all the way in. He shut the van door, as gingerly as possible, and went around to the drivers side.

Garret was already thinking of how to address his captive in his mind. There were hundreds of nomens running through his head but he settled on lowlife for the time being. The lowlife was making some groaning noises in the back but was still completely unconscious. He started the van and pulled out of the alley, aiming for Pigtown. He was 15 minutes away from his first act of vengeance as a civilian and deep inside, he couldn't have been happier. Most people would have some self doubt and crisis of conscience. Thoughts would be swirling around and most would find themselves needing to go to the bathroom. I don't know what it is about that but times like this, people actually need to use the restroom. Not Garrett, he had survived intense operational situations, much worse than this, and had to make split decisions that could cost him and his company life or death. Garrett was in complete control and he credited it to the excellent planning, tempo, and execution. He didn't need to deviate once so far and he intended on keeping that going forward. This planning and execution process is ingrained into all special operators.The risks are discussed and mitigated before they become barriers to success.

When he arrived at the abandoned housing project, Garrett parked in front. *I'll unload the trash, and then go park somewhere down the block under a streetlamp to avoid any suspicion.* He backed up almost right to the front door and got out. When he opened the rear door of the Volkswagen, he realized the shit stain had been tossed around a little while he was driving. He had a bloody nose, disheveled clothes, and wasn't in the same position when he loaded him. He checked to see if It was still breathing and was somewhat relieved to hear a cough as he shifted It onto Its back. He ripped his captive out of the van by the feet, head banging hard on the tailgate and sidewalk. Garrett dragged him through the front door, down the hall, and to the room he had set up. He took Scott to the chair, lifted him up under the arms and placed the limp body there. Using the gorilla tape he stashed on the table, he taped his arms and legs to the chair and then taped his mouth with a small rag soaked in chloroform, ensuring to leave the nose free to breath the stifling air encapsulating the room. He had no idea what it must taste like but he wasn't taking any chances of him waking up while he worked.. After he secured the scumbag to the chair, he went back out and parked the van. When he returned the real fun was about to start.

Garrett took some time to revel in the moment. He looked around the room and made mental pictures of what he saw. His first impression was the dingy, peeling, grey-toned paint that anchored the room he was in. The windows were so filthy that the light, filtering through the haze, cast shadows like hand puppets on the wall.

There must have been some sort of leak from the apartment above because the ceiling appeared like a scene out of a horror movie with paint dripping down. The light fixture, which didn't work because there wasn't any electricity, was missing its glass cover. The two exposed incandescent bulbs sticking out sideways, appeared like the eyes of a malevolent spirit peaking out from the dripping ceiling surrounding them.

The smell in the room is what gave Garrett the biggest mental note. Other than the obvious overwhelming musty smell of mold, there was an overtone of hundreds of cigarettes that were put out and smoldering to the filter. That gut wrenching smell of old, used cigarettes that repulses people. Like being around a well used ash tray. Garrett thought it was odd that he didn't see a single cigarette butt laying around. How in the hell does a smell permeate through an apartment like that when there aren't any physical signs ...it really was baffling. Evidently the smell of used cigarettes has staying power when in an enclosed space. Garrett looked over at the nasty being in the chair and decided it was time to get to work. He wanted to be out of the warehouse, in fact the entire area, before the twilight of dawn. He made one more check on Scott's vitals before he engaged. All was well and the table was set for a supper that neither of them would ever forget.

First, he took the garden loppers off the table and checked them one more time. He found an old, discarded piece of lumber and took a nice chunk out of it with the shears. He was satisfied with the sharpness and immediately went to work on the right hand. Starting with the thumb, he set the open loppers to encapsulate a bit of the thenar tissue. Using the bottom jaws of the shears, he held steady and brought the two handles together with surprisingly very little effort. The sound he heard reminded him of someone chomping down on a carrot. It was a quick, clean crunch. The loppers were still so incredibly sharp that the flow of blood was delayed, not unlike getting cut with a razor during a shave. A quick, slight pain, followed by a few seconds of nothing before the flow of capillary blood. This was a bit different once the blood started to flow. The chloroform-induced coma ensured Scott's lower heart rate and the pressure of the escaping blood would also be low, meaning less immediate blood loss. The severed princeps pollisis artery, although not squirting all the way across the room, did eject about 1/2 to 1 inch from the opening and a pool of blood was already starting to form on the floor below the arm of the chair.

Garrett set the loppers down and picked up the plumber's torch, pushing the starter to engage the tear-dropped, bluish white flame. He aimed it directly at the phalangeal opening, unfamiliar with how it will affect the area. The heat from the torch, around 3,700 degrees Fahrenheit, immediately cauterized the stump. The smell punched Garrett straight in the nose. It caused a fit of dry heaves. He wasn't expecting any foul smells and certainly wasn't ready for them to affect him that way. He had been in plenty of firefights and was familiar with the smell of cordite.

As a medic, he treated wounded soldiers and could relate to the sights, sounds, and smells of the battlefield. A couple hours in a burn unit, during his medical training, didn't prepare him for this level of intensity. Other than an occasional shrapnel wound from an incoming mortar or RPG, which comes in hot and has the same cauterizing effect, he had never smelled a flame on an open wound. The scent registered immediately and was stored in the area of his brain that kept information like that. From that millisecond onward, he knew he would never forget it. He looked back at the red and blackened stump and noticed that most of the bleeding stopped. Some of the thenar skin had bubbled up in third to fourth degree burns. The area looked a lot like the skin of a chicken breast seared in a pan, skin side down. The pimples where the feathers used to be reminded him of the crisp human skin with the teeny holes where the pores are. A small shiver ran down his back as he thought about how this piece of shit was going to feel when he woke up.

I don't give a flying fuck! He was starting to enjoy it now that he was past the initial unpleasantness. After turning it off, he set the torch back on the table and picked up the loppers to finish his work. He decided to take all the rest of the fingers from the right hand before he cauterized them so he didn't have to go through smelling each one separately. He would work as fast as he could switching from the shears to the torch to minimize the blood loss. He wasn't an anesthesiologist and wasn't sure how long the chloroform would last under such trauma. It was, after all, unorthodox and outside of his purview. He went to the best military medic school in the country but all the topics are condensed and modeled for field work. He recalled being trained to apply clean bandages and lots of saline solution to keep the wounds wet, clean, and not sticking to anything.

The real work is done in a sterile hospital environment because the risk of infection increases exponentially with burns.

Garrett finished up with the right hand and moved to the left. It seemed like an hour passed to complete both hands but he did all of it in less than 20 minutes. He looked down at the blood on the floor and guessed there was about 2-3 pints. "Not bad for a days work and the loss of 10 digits," he blurted out in contentment. He couldn't wait for the next part of the plan. He got the brand out of the bag and started to heat it up to an orange-red before he was ready to put it on Scott's skin. *Where should I place it? The middle of the chest seems like a good place but the middle of the back would be better*, he thought. *If I put it in the back, he will not be able to lay down without a lot of pain. He will have the pain coming at him from all different directions. Pain in the back, pain in the hands, pain will not be just a state of mind. This fuck monster won't be able to get any rest for a long time,* He giggled to himself as he realized how perfect this was all working out. He almost felt like the evil scientist on Bugs Bunny. "Nighty Night Rabbit!", he said out loud as he momentarily slipped away, envisioning the famous, ether-induced scene where Bugs Bunny was trying to run away from the evil scientist, who was chasing and calling after him. It was a classic. He laughed out loud, reminiscing.

After a few minutes of what could be called gloating, Garrett checked the brand and could feel the heat radiating off of it. He set all of this in the ratty, kitchen sink while he cut the monster out of the chair and placed him face down on the bed. He pulled up the back of his shirt and made sure he was still breathing. *Still no need for more chloroform? This is some amazing shit! Why don't they use this anymore for surgery?* Scott was starting to groan a bit more and his legs were moving around. Garrett went to his jacket and pulled out the chloroform infused rag. The smell took his breath away. After removing the duct tape from Its mouth, he held it over the nose and mouth for about 5 more seconds. Scott was right back to an immobilizing coma. Garrett went to the kitchen and brought out the brand. It was now glowing almost orange white. He thought how cool it looked. He picked a place right in the middle of Scott's shoulder blades and pushed the brand on the skin. Immediately it sounded like eggs in a cast iron pan and that horrific smell came back for what he hoped would be the last time. There was actual smoke rising off the skin. He was hypnotized for a couple of seconds as he watched the skin turn white and then darken to a deep, deep red.

He removed the brand, which stuck a little bit into the skin, and there before his eyes was the symbol of everything he worked for while he was in the service. The howling 21st never looked so amazing to him. The dog and the lightening and dagger, brought a well of tears to his eyes. He felt like he accomplished something that he hadn't done in a long time. He got the bad guy and did something truly meaningful to ensure It wouldn't be able to hurt anyone again.

IV

Garrett's discharge was not what he expected. Instead of joy and excitement for the future, he was disillusioned and sad. He wasn't ready to leave the life. It had become all he knew and wasn't sure if there was anything else in the world for him. This is not an uncommon theme among veterans. The technical term for it is institutionalization. This term is used a lot to identify people who have spent many years of their life behind prison walls. It can apply to anyone that spends a large portion of their life doing one thing. The person becomes so isolated from the outside world and immersed in whatever it is their doing, that the idea of doing anything else is foreign to them. They are taken from the microcosmic world they live in and shoved out into the macrocosm of the world. The big picture as people in already high places like to call it. Well at this very moment, Garrett was feeling the effects of institutionalization. It is a scary proposition to know only one thing and be so deeply entrenched in it. He was thrust back into something that is so large, he can't fathom where he fits into it all.

On the train from Ft. Benning to Baltimore, he spent the entire time looking out the window, daydreaming about the jungle and his time there during the Drug Wars. He was recruited into the Jungle Dog group after he finished his 18D final training for duty as a combat medic. It is an intensive course that takes place at Ft. Bragg. Some of the older medics called this "goat school" because part of their training involved the care of a goat in varying degrees of trauma to simulate combat scenarios. Garrett excelled at all of his training and upon his initial enlistment, was assigned to this school after scoring well on the ASVAB; the general test that all enlistments take before they go to their physical evaluation. It allows the recruiter the opportunity to place certain individuals, according to aptitude, into more deeper training based on their test scores and preferences.

Garrett originally wanted to go to pre-med but failed his studies after his second semester due to his horrible grades and extracurricular activities, which included fraternal obligations. He always regretted not finishing college but was glad to find a purpose through the military. He was proud to serve his country in that capacity.

The recruitment into his final unit was an intensive and a highly secretive meeting. He actually signed confidentiality papers and non-disclosures before he was even briefed on the group and its operational mission. After the initial briefing, he was immediately sold because it fit so well with his idea of combat and his vision of what his time in the military should be. He was vehemently against the drugs that were infiltrating and ruining his beautiful country and felt compelled to do something about it. This opportunity was going to stop the problem at its source. Cocaine was a big thing around this time and there was so much product coming into the country that no one could monitor or control the flow. With that in mind, stopping any of it in the middle of the stream was virtually impossible. The Coast Guard was making small dents in the smuggling but there was such a large volume, in so many different places, that the Guards weren't able to stop them all.

The cartels were getting the lay of the land and were making so much money they were willing to use sacrificial lambs in the form of smaller vessels that may have a few pounds to divert the attention of the authorities and smuggle in the larger amounts. The money was flowing so freely that the cartels enlisted naval engineers to design small submersibles that could handle a large payload with only a few crew. These tools were used when they wanted to use the sea routes to bring in tons of product under the darkness of night. They would rendezvous with surface vessels off the coast of Florida and transfer the cocaine for shipment to cities like Miami. It was such a large amount and such a dangerous undertaking that often there would be abandoned drugs washing up along the shores of southern Florida and the Keys in huge loads of bricks wrapped in saran wrap type plastic. It really was a horrible epidemic for this country and Garrett figured he was going to be an integral part of stopping it at the source.

The main mission of the Jungle Dog group was to take a squad of highly trained special operators, insert them into the mountains and jungles of South America, typically in Colombia where the majority of the cocaine was coming from, and stop it at the lab level. This group, consisting of multiple squads would provide both intelligence and tactical operations to accomplish this difficult mission. All of the operators in the group were sent to the army jungle school in Hawaii to gain terrain knowledge and survival skills that would help them subsist in that environment. Most of the members of the group were from middle America and had never even seen a tropical environment before. The jungle training awards them the jungle tab, placed on their left shoulders under their ranger and some of them, their special forces tabs.

This specialized and highly clandestine group was only open to rangers and green berets. The units usually consist of 5-6 people; broken down into a squad leader, medical sergeant, engineer, machine gunner, and a radio operator/signalman. All of the operators in the group were specialists that may be trained in explosives/EOD, small arms, and enemy arms. Everyone receives brief cross training, to be redundant in all of the positions. Each individual squad is sent to different areas of the country with large rucksacks full of all the gear they would need to sustain the group for about 2 weeks, which was the normal operating rotation. 2 weeks in this terrain was enough to feel like years of hard labor. Humping 100+ pound rucksacks over mountainous terrain, in well over 95 percent humidity put a lot of wear and tear on the body. It was not unlike running an ultramarathon and not being able to get more than an hour or two of sleep at a time.

The squad usually broke down further after entering the jungle and finding a good observation post near one of the thousands of labs that proliferated the region. The observation post could have been as simple as a hoard of trees with some added camouflage, to a dug out pit with a poncho for a roof. The idea was to have two people constantly manning the post with binoculars and a radio, providing real time intelligence to the rest of the group. Gathering information like how large the area was, how many workers, how many security cartel members and shift times were all relevant and critical in formulating a tactical plan to destroy the lab. Sometimes the squad would merely record information, which would then be relayed back to the main command. Other times the fluidity of the operation would allow for immediate action.

This was the life that Garrett signed on for and spent the better part of 2 years working on. In fact, there wasn't a lot of furlough, so saying this really was his entire life was not entirely wrong. Rotating in and out for 2 weeks at a time, in quite different areas, helped him acquire a very refined discipline. The work with his team, or more realistically, his "blood and sweat" brothers was all he knew for that entire time. He ate, slept, and breathed this life. That is why, when he left it, there was a vacuum created that needed to be filled with something. Oddly enough, it turned out to be a little bit of what he was already good at.

When Garrett arrived back home, he only spent a couple weeks at his parents home and found a place closer to the city in a part of south Baltimore called Brooklyn Park. It was a nice neighborhood in the suburbs close to the usual shopping centers and schools but far enough away from the city to be sheltered from the abhorrent crime areas. Most of the people in the neighborhood were middle class white Americans that worked hard and lived for their weekends. The bingo hall was down the street and there were restaurants within hiking distance that would serve just about any type of food you might want. Garrett was happy to be able to have his own place away from his parents and the north end of the city. There were too many Jews in that area for Garrett and his deep seated German heritage and dislike for those people kept him yearning to get out. He managed to let the basement level of a single family home from some acquaintances he knew from school. It had a separate bedroom and even an open floor planned kitchen/dining/living space. There was access to the laundry area and some storage in the rear. He had his own private entrance and all in all, it met his immediate needs: Privacy, Seclusion, and most importantly, Peace. He spent the first couple of weeks helping around the house. As part of his rental agreement, a verbal one between friends, he was obliged to do a little yard work and help out with the trash cans when he could. Other than that, he was on his own for the first time in what felt like decades. It both terrified and excited him. He didn't have any immediate plans but knew that he should start looking for work because the money he had saved wasn't going to last forever.

Garrett saw an ad in the paper for a batch maker at DAP, inc. down on North Point Boulevard in Dundalk. It wasn't far from his grandparents house and he hadn't seen them in about a decade. He decided to take a trip to the company and apply. When he finished he thought he might take a ride over to his grandparents to catch up and say hello. He decided that an unannounced visit might not be the best idea because of the old fashioned values and because he was somewhat of an unfamiliar face. He didn't want to impose on his grandparents and new they would feel obligated to entertain if he showed up. This was the values of that generation and he just didn't want to be like a prodigal child showing up after all those years and expecting to be entertained. He opted to see how it goes at the job and then formulate a plan to visit if it all worked out.

The following week he found himself alone on the second deck of the DAP manufacturing plant in what seemed like a cloud of white dust working one of the tens of hoppers that fed powdered gypsum and other dry bags to the mixers down below. The company made caulk of varying types as well as drywall compounds that were all sent to distributors to feed the DIY retail stores like Home Depot, Lowes, and Hechinger. Garrett's job was pretty easy going. It was the 80 pound bags by the pallet load that were the hard part. Luckily, there was a forklift on the floor that he used to take pallets of bags at a time, wearing a paper suit and respirator, to cut one bag at a time and send them down the hopper to be mixed with other wet and dry chemicals that would eventually make either the caulk of the day or drywall compound that fed the several lines on the ground floor.

Mexican immigrants and local women would man the lines, which in conjunction with a conveyor belt, would assemble the products from tubes and tubs to covers, shrink wraps, and finally lids and boxes. All the while a single forklift driver would either be feeding the lines with empty tubes at the beginning where the lead operator was, or tubs. At the rear of the lines would be the lids and boxes where the product would go through a glue machine and finally be placed on a pallet by another immigrant to be whisked away and taken to a different part of the warehouse for palletization and storage. Tractor trailers came to be loaded and disembark for all corners of the country. This was the daily flow that Garrett was getting accustomed to.

He worked the midnight shift, as the factory worked 3 shifts, 7 days a week. He found the life to be quite peaceful as long as he was following the recipe for the hoppers of the day. He liked to take his breaks out back where some of the locals would go to smoke cigarettes. It overlooked the train tracks that served this industrial part of the east Baltimore suburbs. He would sometimes converse with some of the low class Dundalk girls that came out for a break but mostly kept to himself. The management liked his hard work and dedication and for the most part left him unsupervised, especially considering the midnight shift and it's skeletal staffing. Garrett was content and figured this was a good way to keep money coming in and formulate a plan that might take him into the next 3-5 years.

It was during one of his lunch breaks that he overhead some of the other english speaking Dundalk crowd talking about a news article in which someone named Scott Finlay had just been released from jail and was a two time offender with a sexual assault charge. He walked over to the group of women and asked to see the article himself. Reading silently, while the hens cackled, he also noted that the article was written with the voice of someone who was appalled at the idea of releasing someone with this record. They also appeared disillusioned with the justice system in Baltimore. This fucking piece of shit had several assaults and batteries as well as auto theft charges. One that caught his eye was the robbery with a pistol. He knew this guy was a complete scumbag and was starting to feel the author's anguish at seeing such a lax in judgement from our judicial superiors. It really was a laughing stock and Garrett started getting angry at the idea of someone like this walking around his neighborhood and wreaking havoc with the people that he grew up with and cared about. He decided right at that moment to see if there was something he could do to remedy this situation. He drove home after his shift with a whole new perspective about the trajectory of his life and his purpose in this world.

V

Hazel Washington was an 82 year old retired nurse that lived in the west Baltimore neighborhood of Druid Hill for most of her life. She, like most people her age, wanted to spend the rest of her time on this earth in peace and prosperity. She deserved as much. She spent a tireless career working at Johns Hopkins in every ward in the hospital treating patients, giving them hope in times of desperation, and feeding and caring for their every need. Why did this beautiful black woman have to be subjected to the degradation of her once important neighborhood only to be afraid to walk down the very street she played on as a child.

Every day was the same for this retiree. She woke early, as most people her age don't sleep much anyway, around 5:00. She went to the kitchen and made herself a cup of Chock Full of Nuts coffee while she went to the bedroom to dress. Outside her front window was one of those abhorrent lots that was occupied almost 24 hours by the drug dealing niggers that scourged that place. She would just shake her head and try to focus on the positive things she hoped to accomplish that day. Deciding on which wig to wear was as simple as looking at what day of the week it was. If it wasn't Sunday, Shiloh Baptist Church day, she opted for a simple curly flat back that was a brilliant orange. She liked it because it went well with the tone of her skin. She saved her black bouffant variant for Sunday, which cost her a week's wages back in the day, to look her best for Jesus. She couldn't recall having ever missed a sermon on Sunday from good reverend Lucas. She remembers going to the same church and Sunday school from the time she was 8 years old. That was about the time her parents moved into the row home that she still occupies to this day. Reverend Lucas was not the preacher back then but he is the true leader of the church she follows today.

This morning she was going to spend time and fry up some bacon and eggs. Normally a cup of coffee and toast with jam was sufficient because her biggest meal was supper. Hazel never married and didn't have any kids. She adored her nieces and nephews and decided that God had provided those lovely creatures for her to spoil instead. She was OK with that and was sure that God's plan for her didn't include a family of her own. As a matter of fact, just last month, she made an appointment with a lawyer to make out a final will that would ensure her estate would be passed on to her beautiful nieces and nephews. She didn't see them often because they all moved to Pennsylvania when her sister got married. She talked on the phone with them at least once a month and enjoyed her visits when they were able to come during their summer break from school.

Growing up in the shadow of Druid Hill Park was something she was very proud of. Ever since she was a young girl she remembers playing there and zipping through the park on her metal wheeled roller skates before her mother called her in for dinner. She was only a couple of blocks away and most of her friends lived within the confines of the same few blocks. This is how it was in those days. Your closest friends were basically neighbors that you went to school with. No one could afford a car so the distance to travel for entertainment was cut as short as one could walk to do anything. Living near the park also meant easy access to the zoo. They both convinced their parents to get them yearly passes and almost every weekend you could find them walking around in the zoo in amazement for all the unique creatures that God created.

There were days, when she got older, she looked forward to the quarter she got from her father to take the bus downtown and back. There was, usually, just enough left over to get a fountain soda. School was only a couple of blocks away, church was only a block, and the best place to play was only a couple of blocks away. Now when she was punished or confined to the block radius of her neighborhood she just gave her parents the ho hum and roller skated over to her friend Latisha's.

She set down her breakfast fork when she started to think about her and a tear fell from her cheek. Latisha passed away a few years ago and she was her best friend...for the last 70 years! They did everything together except work. When they both had time together they were either cooking, listening to records, or going to church. Baptists love to go to church several days a week. The midweek service is called bible study. It is a bit less formal, if that is even possible, than the Sunday service. The group of about 25 men and women usually meet in one of the Sunday school classrooms in a circle of chairs. Hazel and Latisha usually brought 99 percent of the snacks and sometimes meals for the Wednesday evening meetings but that was more for selfish reasons than anything. Latisha claimed she suffered from "the sugar", low blood sugar, and had to eat every couple of hours. The reality is that both of them were obese and probably had pre diabetes. Turns out it killed her too early. She was 78 when the good Lord called her to him. Hazel had a hard couple of years after that. Other than her family in Pennsylvania, she didn't have anyone and now her life was a solitary slug through.

She finished her breakfast and meticulously cleaned and put away all of the dishes. Today she decided she was going to take a bus to the harbor and walk around. She hadn't been downtown in ages and wanted to see how much it had changed after all of the construction.

As with any waterfront city, there is always a couple of budget line items that were dedicated to maintenance and capital expense projects to keep the place modern and fresh. Baltimore is no different and the city leaders were interested in the tourist dollars that bring people to the grandeur and beauty of the waterfront. One of the new restaurants in HarborPlace was Hard Rock Cafe, which was built inside the cavity of the old power plant that fed electricity to the entire city and surrounding suburbs. Since the transition of the electrical grid to nuclear power way out in Turkey Point, the vacant building was the talk of many developers. The winning bid went to the Hard Rock franchise. The inside was quite a spectacle and Hazel was not just interested in that but the giant bookstore, Barnes and Noble, that took over the large space adjacent to that. She figured she could spend the entire day exploring this new area and still not have seen all of the inside. After getting herself ready for the day and loading her bag full of necessities and snacks, she rolled out of the decrepit street and headed for the bus stop.

She spent the entire day strolling through the shops along HarborPlace. It wasn't a familiar site to her but she enjoyed the crowds and watching people going through their daily lives. A couple of times she plopped down on one of the hundreds of benches along the waterfront promenade and took a break with one of the snacks she brought. The thought of all those people in such close proximity to each other and not having a clue about what they were thinking or a single care for anyone else around them, fascinated Hazel. How could so many people be together in the same place and not even acknowledge their presence with a "hello" or simple courtesy of a nod in their direction? It saddened her thinking about how society had changed and how self absorbed people had become. She didn't realize the magnitude of people that came to this beautiful place to spend their vacations or even just the day. She watched as people plied their arts and crafts along the walkways leading to and from the main buildings. She marveled at the boats along the yacht club and wondered what they all were thinking as they looked back from the deck of their vessels into the crowd of masses. It was ironic that she was sitting there watching people that were sitting where they were also just watching people. The watcher is the watched while enjoying the beautiful weather that God provided for her amusement that day.

She truly felt humbled in the midst of it all and grateful that she was able to be even a little part of it for the time she was there.

Towards the evening, she made her way around the harbor to the old power plant and decided to take supper in the Hard Rock Cafe's restaurant before heading over to the bookstore to settle in for some perusing. It takes a lot of energy to walk around in the sweltering heat, next to a reflecting body of water. You never realize how tiring it is until you sit down to take a rest. As she sat there waiting for her food to arrive she decided, fatefully and unbeknownst to her, to take a rain check on the bookstore and make her way back home after supper. From the plethora of usual items on the menu, she decided on a salad and some fried coconut shrimp. She figured she could treat herself considering she rarely makes her way to the city and this was a special occasion. After she ate and settled her bill, she made her way to the bus stop for the not too long trip back to Druid Hill.

When she got off the bus at Clifton, across from the park, she crossed the street and headed down the couple of blocks towards her house. When she got close, she heard the racket that was going on across the street at the empty lot behind the refuse station. There was a 55 gallon drum there that the local bums used during the winter to keep themselves warm. The police never seemed to mind as long as the neighbors weren't making a fuss or complaining about the noise.

Tonight was different. The fire was lit in the middle of summer and there was a crowd of the same hoodlums and drug dealers that she always noticed there. Their loud voices carrying across the lot coupled with the breaking of bottles just got under her skin this evening. She also noticed that the usual crowd of homeless bums that inhabited the area were gone. It was just a bunch of useless, drug-dealing hoodlums looking for trouble and Hazel wasn't going to have any of it tonight. She was tired and wanted to go to bed. She did her best to ignore the distraction and headed for her front door. After she got herself settled for the night, she decided to open the windows and get some fresh air. The noise from across the street was still amping up and now they had a boom box playing some of that music that she couldn't stand. She called it jigaboo music. This was the last straw before she called the authorities. She decided to go over there and say something to these punks because this was her neighborhood and she wasn't going to be intimidated. She put on her robe and grabbed her purse, which was a habit every time she walked out of the house. It contained her keys.

She marched over to the lot and screamed for everyone's attention. "Hey y'all! I came from across the street and its getting late. I'd appreciate ya'll could turn the music down and keep it quiet. Some of us tryin to go to bed and this ain't gonna work!" From the crowd of dark characters, one emerged, defiant and started to curse Hazel,"Yo nigga! Yo, u gotta lotta nerve comin over hir disturbin us! Gon back and min ya own Godam biness ya fat Biyotch!"

"Well I never! yung man I certainly ain't gonna take it from you!" and with that, the young thug gave a smile, showing the few gold teeth he had glittering in the glow of the fire and walked over to Hazel getting right in her face. Without a flinch and the smell of Mickey's on his breath he spit right in the woman's face...The absolute horror and disrespect! *How dare you*, Hazel thought. She was so shocked at the action that she didn't even realize that he had a hold of her purse and was trying to pull it off her arm. When she put up the least resistance he pushed her to the ground. She held onto her purse with dear life and was soon to regret that. He started at her with a kick to the arm that would make a soccer player proud. The crunch of her bones said it all as she let out a loud cry and yelp.

"Help me dear Jeezuz, Help! Help!, Help Me Gawd!"

"He ain't herd u bitch! how u like me now mutha fucka! Now leggo that purse Bitch!" She struggled as long as she could but the pain from her fractured arm was too overwhelming and she lost control of it. Finally gaining control of the purse, he threw it over to the crowd around the fire. Then the monster decided to go to work on the woman laying there without the slightest regard for her life. He kicked and kicked and kicked at this poor woman's ribs until she finally fell unconscious. He gave one last punt to her head as he backed up and wound down like he was kicking a field goal for the Ravens. He felt the woman's head bounce around and heard the creaking of her neck bones. A small trickle of blood began to form around her mouth and nostrils. He kicked the poor, defenseless old woman so hard in the ribs that one of them broke loose inside and punctured a lung.

He took one final look at her lying on the ground in front of him and hocked a loogie all over her robe. As she lay there he yelled back over his shoulder to the rest of the crowd and said.'Yo ya'll, lez roll!" And they all, casually as if nothing had even happened, strolled down the street back towards the park. They left the scene with the woman lying in the lot, next to the burning can, with an emptied purse. The only other sounds were of cars passing on the main road off in the distance. A solitary street light was lit and buzzing with the sounds of the sodium-vapor lamp about half a block away. The only thing left was an impending silence, as all of the neighbors had gone to sleep for the night.

Lamar Jenkins was a typical west Baltimore, drug dealing thug. His mouth was always bigger than his ability to back it up and most of the people he hung out with were carbon copies; Myna birds; little ducklings following their mother around. They all dropped out of high school during senior year (that tells you how stupid they really were...How can you get all the way to the end and just quit before its over) and spent most of their time hanging out in vacant lots, selling drugs and drinking 40s of Mickey's malt liquor. "Yo nigga! look cross da strit! C dat homie! Dat nigger wanna git his ass kik'd!" was a typical call from either lot and the ebonics flowed like ambrosia. In reality, it is such a smooth way to talk and easy on the ears to hear. The downside is that it shows the absolute dregs of society and lack of a proper education that most of these "homies" sorely needed. The truth is, math was their only friend and the basic grammar school type at that. How much was an ounce? A fifth? A quarter? What did each one cost? These were the important math and economical figures that mattered on the streets. Learning algebra and macroeconomics was not high on their priority list. They were oblivious to anything outside of their little microcosm. As they prospered, the rest of the neighborhood felt the pinch. Property values go down, cops just give up because they are all back on the streets due to prison overcrowding, and the neighbors are too scared to say anything because of the threat of retaliation. These assholes basically run the place at the ripe age of 14 to 18.

Lamar had a bit of a psychopathic streak in him and it shined hard tonight. He was walking with his friends back towards Druid Hill Park with a stranger's wallet in his pocket. He had just beat on old fat woman to death and took her purse because she came out of her house and disrespected him in front of his homies. He was having a good time showing off and drinking 40s next to a fire that his friends had started in an old can. They were singing along to some hip hop music and minding their own business when this woman had to come and ruin the good time. He gave her a what she came looking for and kicked the living shit out of her.

He grew up in a typical west Baltimore household with a single mother, never having actually met his father. He had 5 siblings of varying ages. He was the oldest of the brood and never took to the family life. He was drawn more to the gangs in the neighborhood that always seemed to have some money in their pockets and always carried some heat in the form of a semiautomatic pistol. At 18, Lamar had been in and out of the juvenile justice system and spent a few days in city lockup as an adult for minor drug charges. His biggest charge was as a juvenile when he and some friends decided to boost some cars in the city and were driving around shooting off their guns into neighborhood houses. Luckily none of the bullets struck anyone. The police chased them in a Honda Accord for 20 blocks until they finally crashed into a light pole while trying to make a high speed turn. I guess they wanted to act out a scene from Fast and Furious. Without the proper training in those types of high speed maneuvers, it usually means a wreck is on the horizon. Lamar was taken into custody and charged with the worst of it because he was the oldest in the bunch and he was the one holding the gun when they were all finally arrested. He wasn't driving but he was the one the courts felt held the most responsibility. He spent the better part of 2 years in juvenile hall for that one. Of course he was given probation when released and that just added to the subsequent charges and additional time with each new conviction.

Lamar didn't live for tomorrow. His only concern was today, right this minute. Within an hour of some booze and music, he and his friends forgot all about Hazel and the confrontation. They crossed the park heading for home, trying to figure out where to score the next stack of cash. Little did Lamar know, or care, that his future was bleak.

VI

Garrett's childhood was not what you would call typical. His father worked for the government and this came with its own set of challenges. Most postings brought very little salary increase and the only way to really get ahead was to apply for a promotion to a higher position. These promotions usually involved moving from one place to another. For a young adolescent this can be devastating, because you are constantly changing schools. It is hard to keep a core group of friends when you are constantly moving.

At that age, keeping in touch is usually just walking down the street to a friends house or meeting at the playground. Writing letters to a friend after you have left the area is more of a chore than an enjoyment. So Garrett was accustomed to making a new group of friends every 2-3 years. During his childhood, Garrett moved around the DC metro area in a radius of about 50 miles. A couple of years in Virginia, a few in Maryland, and a good chunk moving to different sections of downtown Washington.

Being an only child was great for his parents because they only had to hear one set of complaints when it was time to pack up and move to the next town. One silver lining happened when Garrett was a teenager and his father took a foreign service post in southeast Asia. It was a 4 year gig in the Philippines. He spent the better part of his middle school years there and never once bothered to learn about the culture. He was insulated from the poverty surrounding him by being enrolled in the International School of Manila. Mostly upper class filipinos and foreign dignitary's children. It actually made him feel like he was royalty. He did struggle though, because most of his teachers were locals and he had trouble understanding them and their broken english. He wound up getting into altercations with some of the richer kids that he felt inferior to.

All in all, he wound up enjoying what time he spent there and looked back on his time with fondness. It also helped on his enlistment form that he had experience living in a foreign country. But once again, it was time to move on and his parents brought him back to the states. They finally settled in a northern suburb of Baltimore called Aberdeen. There was an army base nearby that his father was somehow affiliated with. He liked being able to go to the commissary and PX with his mother. There was always a great selection of candy and toys for him to indulge in and his parents allowed him that latitude because they knew he suffered with the lifestyle.

When he was in elementary school his teachers would send notes home about his behavior and inability to focus during class participation. His mother enlisted the help of several therapists along the course of his childhood and eventually he was tested for IQ. It turned out that his was fairly high. It explained the detachment from classroom functions and when questioned about it he often replied that he was bored. He did well on all of the standardized tests and was obviously absorbing the information he was being taught. He was on par with the rest of the class when it came to his reading and comprehension skills but for some reason always had his head in the clouds, daydreaming of being somewhere else. That was a terrible distraction to his teachers. It turned out later in his army career to be an asset. His ability to compartmentalize things was invaluable in the field and during training.

Garrett finished high school in Aberdeen and was shipped off to a private college in the hills of Tennessee, not far from Johnson City. He wasn't particularly excited about going to the school but if his father was going to pay for it this was where he was going. During one of their many moves, Garrett's father became acquainted with a well off family in South Carolina. It was the last place he saw before their move to the Philippines. This business friend of his father's was an evangelical christian and sent all of his kids to this school, nestled in the foothills of eastern Tennessee. It was a fundamental christian college and there were requisite bible courses for any of the degrees. His father considered it to be a well rounded education and wanted his son to have every opportunity he could.

He spent his first semester away from home getting acquainted to life without his parent's rule. Being a good student helped his academic transition but he struggled socially. He rebelled against the christian roots of the college and found some like-minded friends living in his dormitory. It wasn't long before they were all as thick as thieves and getting into trouble. Garrett was even placed on academic probation for the last couple months of the semester because of his falling grades.

When he came back after the winter break, things only got worse. His friends and he decided they were going to start their own fraternity, which was forbidden by the fundamentalist school, and things went from bad to worse. His grades plummeted as low as they could go and he was once again placed on academic probation. When the school year ended, he decided it was a waste of his father's money to continue. He was over 18 now and wanted to make some life decisions for himself. He decided on enlisting into the service. He wasn't sure what branch and found some recruiters that were more than willing to introduce him to life in the military. He went to the naval recruiter the next day and explained he just finished his first year of college. He indicated his major was pre-medicine. The recruiter explained the wonderful world of the Hospital Corpsman and their distinguished accomplishments in the field of battle. He watched a 20 minute film on the Navy Seals and their program. He thanked the recruiter and went right next door to the Army.

After an hour sitting with him, watching another film on the Special Forces, he was hooked. He was enamored with the Green Beret and what it stood for. It was going to be a long road in a mountainous, uphill battle but he was resolute. He signed up that very day to a 4 year enlistment in the Army. He was guaranteed a spot in their basic medical course but would have to pass the selection process to become a Ranger and ultimately a Green Beret. That was how the rest of his life began and he couldn't have been happier. He was on the bus the next day to take his ASVAB. The acronym was typical of military speak. It stood for the Armed Services Vocational Aptitude Battery. The results of this test helped determine where you would be a good fit in terms of work. All soldiers go through boot camp. After basic training, those that scored well on the ASVAB are sent to specialized schools, which they show an aptitude or ability to learn. Garrett was on his way to combat medic training.

VII

Scott Finlay was taken to Harbor Hospital when the ambulance arrived in Pigtown, to answer a call for a man missing all of his fingers. The crackheads that helped him outside the warehouse used one of the neighborhood bar's phones to call 911 and report the odd fellow that showed up on their street, with bloody bandages on his hands and an odd burn on his back. Shirtless and howling in pain, he was given some morphine by the attending paramedic that showed up. It made him feel real good. He was placed on the gurney and loaded into the ambulance while the police were trying to get some information from him. When the morphine kicked in it was lights out again for the 3rd or 4th time in 24 hours. The only difference this time was that he didn't seem to have a care in the world that he was missing his fingers. He wasn't used to the potency of the morphine and slept most of the way to the hospital.

The nature of the scene caused some alarm with the patrol officers and the sergeant on duty made a call to the southern district for help from a detective in the violent crimes unit. There wasn't anyone there that day so the call was routed to the central district where Detective Cecilia Dower answered the phone. After hearing the information from the sergeant, she wanted to see the man for herself and try to get some more information from him about the assault and eventual amputation of his fingers. She leaned over her cubicle to her partner, Detective Sergeant Paul Young at his desk and busily typing away on his last report for the day.

"Hey Paul, I jus got de stranges call from the duty sergeant at Southern and you won't believe what he jus tol me."

"What dat Cel? We gonna git some more work put on us dat we can't handle?"

"Not necessarily, I'm more interested in dis one cause of how bizarre it is. He say some dude was found outside a abandoned housing project in Pigtown wit all his fingers cut off. You ever heard any weird shit like dat?"

"Hell no! Now run dat by me gain." So Cecilia told him everything the desk sergeant told her and they were both so intrigued at the case they decided to drop what they were doing and head right over to Harbor Hospital and talk to this guy.

Detective Sergeant Young was a 54 year old black man that spent the last 25 years on the Baltimore City Police force grinding away at whatever was thrown at him. He wasn't super ambitious and wasn't interested in a college degree. So he figured if he was going to get off the street and out of uniform, he was going to have to put the work in to make sergeant. It took him about ten years on patrol to finally get the courage to take the test. He passed it on his first try. He had enough time in rate to get promoted but there weren't any open positions yet. All the old timers were trying to put in the time to get their full ride pensions. 20 years was only half the ride. They were all looking for that 30 year mark. Paul knew it so he figured he would wait it out.

In the meantime he took a job in the narcotics division until a slot could open up in homicide. That was his real passion. That is until he made it to the violent crimes unit. He realized after a couple of weeks that he was exactly where he wanted to be. He was partnered with Detective Dower when he arrived and they spent the last 10 years working together. It was like a marriage at work. They knew each other so well that eventually they spent a lot of the holidays together. Paul was a dedicated employee to the police force and was waiting patiently for his time to come so he could retire on his full ride. Only 5 more years to go.

Cecilia was 41 and it took her 10 years to make Detective. She took the college route at night school while she worked patrol during the day. Her degree in criminal justice was one of her proudest achievements. Her and her husband decided that children weren't in the cards so they both focused on their careers and their beautiful marriage of 22 years. They lived vicariously through their nieces and nephews and were perfectly happy living their lives and provided enrichment through their work. Cecilia adored her work relationship with Paul and they were both known around the office as the clowns.

When they were together there was always laughter and levity. It was as if God had a hand in putting them together because whatever one lacked in the field, the other covered. Cecilia was the kind hearted and open person that was great at eliciting information from people that never really intended on giving it up. Paul was the heavy handed "bad cop" in the scenario and was great at restoring order when it was lost and controlling the scenes and patrol officers. When they heard about this odd case, both of them were in 100 percent..

When they arrived at the hospital, they checked in with the nurse, only to find that he still hadn't been transported to a room and was awaiting surgery. They had to go in and clean up the stumps that were left where his fingers used to be. If they wanted to wait they would have to do so in the waiting room, otherwise the nurse wouldn't mind giving them a call. They both looked at each other and decided they weren't going anywhere but right where they were. "Hey Cel, you hungry? I know a great place down de road in Brooklyn. We could go and get some crab cakes while we waitin?"

" Hoowee! That sound good to me boy! Les go. Wait a minute I wanna give de nurse my card so she can call me soon as he wake up!" She handed the duty nurse her card with instructions to call her immediately when he is stable enough to talk and answer questions. It is important to any junvestigation involving a crime, to get answers as soon as possible because the details have a habit of slipping away in harmony with the passing of time. And every good detective knows that the devil is usually in the details. Paul and Cecilia went out to the car and drove down the road to get something to eat to fuel up for the adventure they were sure they were about to embark on.

It was about 2 1/2 hours later when Cecilia's phone started to buzz with an unknown number. It was the duty nurse explaining that the patient had finally gotten out of surgery and was being admitted into one of the rooms in the surgery ward. It would be about another hour before he was fully awake and they would be able to question him. It was everything they could do to exhibit patience. They had to wait another hour, so they got back into the car and headed to the hospital. They would rather be waiting there and not miss a single opportunity to have a chat with this guy about one of the strangest things either of them had witnessed in their entire careers.

The nurse came down the hall to the quaint waiting area on the surgery ward, where the detectives were both napping after their crab cake smorgasbord. She instructed them that he was heavily sedated but they were welcome to go in and try to ask him some questions. Cecilia had been in lots of hospital rooms but when she went in this one, she saw the rack over the bed and her first thought was a middle ages torture chamber, deep in a dark, dank dungeon.

Scott had both of his arms in slings. His arms were gently resting down towards his legs but slightly elevated so that they were above his heart. The nurse explained that this was to help with the thumping pain associated with this type of trauma. The bed was surrounded with all types of beeping monitors and bags of IV fluids. There was also a tube coming out from the side of the bed to a clear plastic bag hooked on the bedpost. It appeared to be about half full of a straw-colored liquid which she surmised to be urine. "Ma'am, is he conscious enough to answer our questions?" asked Paul. He had been so absorbed with the instruments and machinery, when he looked over he noticed that the patient was out cold.

"He should be but I can't guaranteed that he will be able to stay awake the whole time. As I said, he is heavily sedated for the pain and discomfort." Paul said thank you and they both walked over to the side of the bed. "Sir!" shaking the man on the hips as she announced, "Sir! Sir, what is your name?" The nurse said his name was on the wristband that the hospital attaches to verify identification for a variety of things. Giving medication is probably one of the most important reasons for this ID. In this case, no one knew his name so the wristband said, "John Doe". Cecilia knew that was such a cliche but continued to try to wake him up. The sooner she could get some answers, the sooner she could move on with the investigation.While this was going on, Paul was having a side conversation with the nurse to see if there was any more information he might be able to gain. The woman was not there when he arrived in the ER so she suggested he start there. She was one of the nurses on the ward and only took responsibility for the patient when he came out of the recovery room post op. "Hey Cel, I'm gonna head down to the ER and see if I can get any information from them, OK? I'll see you in a bit..."

"OK Paul but make sure you try to get the paramedics that brought him in. If anyone has some valuable information, it would be them.They the first on the scene."

"Sure enough Cel. See you later alligator!" With that, he slipped out the door to the unit and made his way to the elevator bank. Back in the room, Cecilia continued her efforts to try to wake him up and start questioning him. "Sir!, Sir!" her voice getting louder as she increased her vigorous shaking on the man's hips. "I really need you to try to wake up and help me answer some questions. What is your name, sir?" To her surprise, the patient opened his eyes, which seemed to be a bit glazed over, as would be expected with someone on pain killing opioids. She managed to get a bit of a groan out of him, which she interpreted as someone in an immense amount of pain.

She felt terribly sorry for this guy but needed to stay focused and do her job. "Sir, if you can understand me, shake your head yes." He registered the question and shook his head up and down once. "Sir, my name is Detective Dower. I am with the Baltimore City Police Department. Do you know where you are?" He acknowledged with an up and down shake of the head. He let out what sounded like a very weak yes and Cecilia figured that the combination of drugs and anesthesia from the operation were not helping his verbal responses. "Could you try to tell me what brought you here? Now take your time, I don't want you to feel rushed but it is important that I figure out what brought you here to the hospital. The more information you can give me, the more I will be able to help you."

He was looking around the room and taking in all the information while trying to recount for the detective exactly what led to him lying in a hospital bed. After about a minute of gathering what bit of thoughts he had, he started with what he could remember. With a slow and deliberate demeanor he stated, "My name is Scott Finlay." She was fairly sure she heard that name somewhere but at the moment, it was slipping her mind. He kept going, "Detective, you'll have to forgive me but I really don't recall much. I remember being in a bar on Fort Avenue. I was playing my weekly pool league. When it was over I vaguely remember walking down the hill towards Locust Point, where I live. That is about all I can remember other than waking up in a strange room and my fucking fingers gone. Oh God! What am I gonna do?!" He started sobbing and shaking, which just made his hands hurt worse. The nurse heard the sobbing and came in to check on him.

"Sir, I know it's hard but do you have any more details about when you arrived at your house? It really is important to try and figure out where this all started." Cecilia was an incredibly patient woman and was trying to turn that up with this case. She couldn't image putting herself in his shoes, with the pain and agony, and loss of the use of his hands. She was trying to be as empathetic to the situation as possible but also push him to expand his memory for details. *The devil is in the details*, she thought as she sat across from him in the cardiac chair that most hospital rooms have on wards like this.

"I don't have a fucking clue how or why this happened!", he declared with an increased distress in his voice.

"Do you know of anyone that might want to harm you? Were you in any fights recently with anyone? Did you get in a fight at the pool league?"

"NO! NO! nothing like that. It is just a bunch of neighborhood people getting together to let of some steam and drink. All of the people in that bar are my friends. Sure, we get into heated arguments sometimes but nothing that would cause me to loss all my fucking fingers!AWWWWWWH! Dear God, what am I going to do now? I can't even take care of myself like this? What is going to happen to me?" Just then, the nurse was adjusting the dosemeter hooked to the morphine drip. She clicked the button and watched as the liquid slowly made its way down the IV tubing to the heparin lock he already had inserted into his arm. He immediately rolled his eyes into the back of his head and dozed off. Other than the whirring of the machines, the room felt eerily quiet after that.

"You should probably go. This man needs to rest and the added stress your creating isn't going to help his recovery" said the nurse.

"I know ma'am but I ain't gonna be able to help him if I can't get answers to some simple questions. I need to get some more details about yesterday evening so I know where else to start looking. You can certainly appreciate that, can't you ma'am? Anyway, I guess I'm not gonna get anymore out of him today. When he wakes, please let him know that I'll come back tomorrow. Let him know I hope he is feeling a little better.Hopefully, we can be more productive with the questions."

" I will do that but again, no guarantees. Until then, you have a great evening detective." With that, Cecilia decided to head down to the ER to meet up with Paul and see what information he was able to get. She took one last look at Scott and grabbed her purse. *This is going to be one wild ride and I am so glad to be on it,* She thought to herself.

She arrived in the ER to the sounds of alarms and the skittering back and forth of tens of doctors, nurses, and technicians all seeming to get somewhere and nowhere all at the same time. She giggled to herself because it reminded her of a show she watched on Discovery channel about bees. She thought how much this moving about reminded her of the bees in a hive and how they all moved and hummed around looking like they weren't doing anything but the reality is they were doing everything. *I guess that's where they got the phrase busy as a bee.* Paul was over in the far corner talking to one of the nurses that was not flitting about the floor. She approached the two of them and Paul immediately looked over and said, "You ain't get much out of him did you? Those drugs can be a problem when it come to questionin."

"Well as a matter of fact, kind sir, I gots a name. He say his name was Scott Finlay. Where we know that name from?"

"Ain't that the guy dat was in the papers for a sexual assault charge on a minor?"

"Holy Shit Paul! Thaz it! I was up there tryin to figure out where I hird dat name. You hit da nail on da head. Dis jus keep gettin better all da time." With that statement and a smirk, she motioned for Paul to finish up so they could get going. She wanted to head over to the crime scene and try to piece together any evidence from there before it got too late. She had a date night with her husband and she didn't want to be late for that. They both headed out to the parking lot, got into their issued Chevy Impala and headed across the bridge to Pigtown.

When they arrived, the crime tape was still up and there there was one sentry posted to keep the area clear until the investigation was completed. Paul walked over to the patrolman and asked, "Yo D. When CSI leave?"

"Bout a hour ago. No one else aint been hir."

"OK man, keep it clear here. We gonna take a look round. Dis hood a bad one, so keep on yo toes OK?"

"OK Sarge!"

"Hey Cel, les take a look round da inside!" Paul opened the door to the hallway, turned the flashlights on their phones, and took a look around. It looked like your typical abandoned job site that are scattered all over the city. Graffiti on the walls and doors, used needles with the orange caps laying all over the ground, and the occasional empty bottle of Mickey's. Or that really cheap vodka they sell for a couple bucks at all the corner package stores in the city.

Some people believe there is a conspiracy in cities like Baltimore.They try to keep the lower class communities drugged and boozed up to keep them under control. If you spend some time there really looking around, you would probably subscribe to that line of thinking. All of the corners seem to be bars and they all have basically the same bottles of liquor they sell as package goods. The side streets and alleys are loaded with drug dealers and it wouldn't take a great distance to find whatever you were in the mood for. Paul and Cecilia are subscribers to this conspiracy and are always at a lack of ways to break that mold.

"Hey Paul, take a look over here! Look a dis doorknob! It look like ders some smired blood on dere."

"Sure do! Go on inside, les take a peek." They both entered the room that Scott was held in and were aghast at what they found. The bloody loppers were still sitting on the table next to the torch and there was still pieces of duct tape all over the chair. Cecilia got on the phone to the lab to ask the CSI unit to come back out and document the room. She was sure no one was in there. The crime scene for the moment was all outside where the victim was found but no one bothered to do a thorough investigation of the warehouse. There were puddles of dried blood under each of the chair's arms. This made Cecilia shiver a little. She just couldn't imagine what would possess someone to torture another human being like that and in that way. The smell of burnt skin and hair was still permeating throughout the room and especially the cover on the makeshift bed lying in the far corner.

Across the river on the south side of town, Garrett was getting his supper ready and sucking down a couple of beers. The morning paper was still folded up on the kitchen table and he was anxious to see if there was any news about the asshole with the missing fingers. With Chris Stapleton's version of "Tennessee Whiskey" playing on his stereo, he was unconsciously led to the cabinet and pulled down a half spent bottle of Jim Beam. With a wince and gasp, he took a nice slug and chased it with his bottle of PBR. He was a Baltimore and what better way to pay some homage to the city than indulge in one of its exports. The beer had been bottled in the city for decades and the winking man was a sign you could run into just about anywhere along the streets.

His steak fajitas were finally done and he already had the flour tortillas sitting on the table. His hunger level was through the roof with all the action he had the last week and he couldn't wait to sit down and read through the paper, searching for any articles that might bring about a new project. The air outside was nice with the sun going down, the cicadas were chirping in the tree outside the window and all of the universe was in order for the time being. Garrett sat there with a smile on his face, determined to enjoy those fajitas.

VIII

Druid Hill was swarming with Baltimore City's finest early this morning, when two of Hazel's neighbors came out for their morning constitutional and ran smack into her, lying on the street behind the refuse station lot. Poor Ms. Johnson fainted right next to Hazel's body and her walking companion left her there to waddle home screaming for someone to "call the POL-EES!" When they arrived, they were able to feel a pulse and tried to rouse her from her unconscious state while waiting for EMS. Her condition looked grave and upon the paramedics assessment, it was deemed important to get her in a cervical collar, mount her on a backboard, and hike her onto a gurney for transport to Mercy Hospital in downtown Baltimore. After starting an IV, which wasn't easy to do on her thick arms, and putting her other obviously fractured arm in a brace, they loaded her up under full lights and sirens with a police escort to the hospital.

Her neurological field tests weren't looking too good and she was in and out of consciousness. She woke one time and tried to pull at the IV in her arm. The attending paramedic was worried about the head and neck trauma so he radioed ahead to the hospital for a specialist to ensure all the bases were covered. When they arrived at the hospital, they were met with the ER team and a full compliment of residents that were visiting from the University of Maryland Medical Campus. They wheeled her into the trauma bay and immediately started their assessment. As the staff scampered about in a seemingly unorganized mess, the X-ray techs doing their work, the neurologist doing his tests, the nurses shouting and scampering back and forth, and the attending physician conducting this pseudo orchestra, Hazel was in the best hands she could be.

After 20 minutes of evaluations, they determined there was a severe closed fracture on her left tib/fib. There seemed to be a fracture of the C2 and C3 spinous processes, and her 7th, 8th, and 9th ribs were fractured and perforated the lower lobe of the left lung. The attending physician ordered a chest set and wanted to insert a chest tube immediately. As he was scrubbing up in the ancillary scrub room, the nurses were prepping Hazel with iodine and sterile paper covers. It is not uncommon to insert a chest tube in the ER but the preferred place is in the OR. It just happened that there wasn't one immediately available because the last surgery just ended and the room was still being sanitized.

With the chest tube set in place, on the table next to the patient and the attending physician scrubbed and suited up, the surgical nurse helped the doctor on with his gloves. He took the scalpel and made a small incision between her 7th and 8th rib directly in line with the curve of the ribs on her left side. He could palpate the broken ribs and inserted his fingers in the small incision to relieve the ribs and put them back into their normal positions. He then took the tube from the tray and inserted it into the incision. With a slight push he was able to penetrate the lung and began suturing the tube in place. In the background, one of the attending nurses hooked the tube up to the bag and released the crimp on the tube. There was an initial rush of blood and fluid into the bag, which signaled a good placement and she placed the bag on the rim of the bed frame. The whole procedure took no more than 20 minutes but an immediate improvement in Hazel's oxygen saturation was noted. Considering the improvement and all the functional testing seemed to pass, Hazel was stabilized and admitted to the ICU for further care.

About 15 miles away in the suburb of Brooklyn Park, Garrett was sitting down to a cold beer and the latest edition of the Baltimore Sun. He browsed the Sports section and was tickled at the box scores. Apparently the Orioles were, again for the thousandth time, in the pennant race. He knew that would be short lived because the past 5 years had shown the same pattern. Make it to the semifinals and choke. He didn't have his hopes up and even considered a bet against them if the odds were right. He was sure they weren't going to make it in the League race. He chuckled to himself and turned the page. An obscure part of the paper contained the police blotter. His eyes got real wide as he explored this small section of the paper and the gears started engaging in the back of his mind. This is where I should be looking to find more scumbags to teach a lesson to.

Nothing crossed his mind this time but he decided that he was going to make this a routine to check every day. He made a mental note of the writer for that column so he could get some inside information if he ever needed it. Miles away, a poor black woman was suffering from a crime she didn't even expect. He could feel the machines humming and beeping in the ICU. He could smell that institutional cleaner that they use to sanitize all the hard surfaces with. He dozed off on the couch with the almost empty beer can in his hand, to the rhythmic tune of a heartbeat on a monitor in his mind for a person that he has never met.

IX

Detective Dower and Detective Sergeant Young were once again asked to take the lead on an investigation into a brutal beating that happened on the North end of the city. When they arrived in their white Chevy Impala with embedded lights, the patrolman lifted the crime scene tape that was blocking off the end of the street adjacent to the refuse station in Druid Hill. Cecilia actually hated to drive in the city and was more than happy to sit in the passenger seat while her work husband, Detective Sergeant Young, took the alpha role and did all the driving. She was happy to man the radio when needed and provide navigational tips much like a backseat driver. This didn't bother Paul because he was used to the same torture from his wife while driving here around town.

They both exited the car and took a brief look around at the scene. The fire had gone out in the can but the embers were still smoldering, emitting a faint wisp of smoke from the top of the can that could be smelled blocks away. It is funny how a clean burning fire doesn't really have a smell and a smoldering fire can be smelled from a great distance. I guess this was exactly what the Dakota Indians were trying to accomplish on the plains when they figured out how to dig a pit in the ground with an adjacent hole for feeding air. The fire was below the surface and had plenty of air to keep it fed. Small sticks were the only necessary fuel and meals could be cooked on it. Undetectable from a distance, the Dakotas were able to survive without giving away their positions to their enemies.

This was the first thing Cecilia noticed when she arrived and asked the officer on the scene about it. *It was the middle of summer for God sake. What was the fire for?* Of course, the patrolman didn't have an answer and left it to the detective to figure it out. Sergeant Young was more interested in witnesses, of which there were few. One of the neighbors across the street, who was a close friend of the victim, was in tears over the knowledge that her beloved friend and church patron was in the hospital on the brink of her life. He tried to calm her down and offer his sympathies while eliciting some information but there was none to give.

All of the witnesses were only aware of the incident after the fact. The only information anyone was able to provide was about the gang of hoodlums that were in the lot the night before causing all kinds of trouble. None of the other neighbors had the guts to face them but Hazel did. She was a stalwart of the community and provided the rock that everyone else used for support in times of trouble. Ms. Johnson, one of her friends that initiated the call to the police, corroborated this story about the problem with the empty lot. Cecilia went to work on this and started to ask around, in a wider radius, about the group of people that were there in the lot that night.

Most of the neighborhood were familiar with the homeless vets that take up residence there during the cold winter nights because of the fire but this was a different group. They were all a bunch of drug dealing thugs that needed to be run off. Finally, about 2 blocks from the scene a young black girl offered up a name for one of the suspected gang members that were there drinking that night. "Lamar", she said. "He name Lamar. I think it Jackson or Jenkins or somfin! Him an dem fools live on da udder side da parc!" Cecilia thanked her for the information, made a note in her moleskin tablet, and headed back to the scene to share the lead with Paul.

She arrived to find Paul bullshitting with one of the patrol officers about the chances for the Ravens this year. "Lamar gonna be better dis yer! He done been hurt too much so he best pull his wait!" Paul was intimating in his ebonic vernacular.

"Yes saw! I gree. He gonna need to put it on em this yea!"

"Paul, aint you two got anythin better to talk bout? We got us a lead and I spect we gonna find em. He known to be on the other side of da park." Cecilia motioned with her hand as she interrupted the two fellows agreeing on the Raven's quarterback.

"Well les git on it!" They headed back to the district office to use the computer and find out who this Lamar was. It didn't take long to pull up a Lamar Jenkins on the screen. Multiple priors and a general piece of shit according to Paul. He made a copy of his picture and decided they should go back and show it to the girl that identified him there.

When they arrived, the girl immediately said yes, without a doubt and that he was a bad "Mo Fo". They both said they appreciated the vote of confidence and would follow up if there were any more questions or they needed her to identify him in a line up. Having already written down an address from his multiple convictions, they only needed to drive around the park to the adjacent neighborhood to find his house of record. A knock on the door was all it took. Lamar, in a stupor from the multiple nights of drinking and druggin finally caught up with him and there was nowhere to run. They asked him a few preliminary questions and then took him into custody so they could crack him down in one of the interrogation rooms set aside in the precinct for just that. Paul was thinking how great it would be to get in there, turn off all the cameras, and go to work on his skinny mother fucker. Professionalism prevented that type of behavior but it wasn't against the law to think or wish it. With a smile on his face, he escorted Lamar to the car and they all drove back to the office for a couple rounds of *Good Cop, Bad Cop.*

It wasn't four hours into a rather uneventful interrogation that Lamar finally caved. The big mouth, all talk son of a bitch gave right in. Sitting alone, isolated, without food and cigarettes, was getting the best of him. He might have been good at putting on airs in front of his posse but when you put him in a room by himself for hours at a time, he isn't worth the expensive clothes on his back. He caved on the fifth hour when he decided he wasn't going to speak. Paul, playing the bad cop, decided he was going to leave him in there for another hour by himself to think about it.

Immediately after Paul left the room, in what felt like days because of the lack of windows or clocks for orientation, Lamar broke down and asked for a cigarette and a coke. This time, Cecilia came into the room with a can of Pepsi, because that was all they had at the moment, and a pack of menthol cigarettes that they keep in a drawer for this exact occasion. She set the Pepsi down on the table and Lamar grabbed it and polished it off in a matter of 4 gulps. He grinned at the cigarette and said, "Yo miss, can I git a lite?" She took a lighter out of her pocket, that she put there from the drawer because she didn't smoke, and gave him a light. "Yo, yo, where I gonna ash?"

"Use the can", she tersely replied and put her hands in her pockets. The Glock 22 she carried was just staring Lamar in the face and he was already anxious, tired, and hung over so his answers were disjointed at best. He laid out the story as well as he could remember and admitted to kicking the lady multiple times in her side and head. After his confession, he was handcuffed and taken across the street to the city jail for processing. He was charged with attempted murder and theft. He only got off with that because the lady didn't die, Paul told him as he was escorted out of the room. As per the usual, Lamar bonded out of city jail the next day on a $50,000 bond. He was so flush with cash from the drug business that his friend "Twiggie" paid the bondsman with $5,000 cash.

Kendall Firth happened to be at central district's front desk talking to the duty sergeant when the day's list of arrests was updated and hung on the wall behind all the plexiglass and wood. He tried to get there every morning around 10 to see what else he could add or write about for his small spot in the Sun weekly paper. There wasn't room on any of the weekend spaces so he was relegated a spot in the weekly run for daily arrests and disposition. It was never intended to be a drawn out editorial on the daily workings of the downtown justice system but it was an account of the actions of the police department for each particular day. This day was no different than the others. The usual drunk and disorderlies, armed robberies, and assault and batteries. But there was one offense on the list that was particularly interesting to Kendall today. Attempted murder on an 80 year old black woman in Druid Hill over the theft of a purse. His excitement grew considering he only sees this type of charge once or twice every couple of months.

Baltimore is riddled with crimes of this nature but they are only caught and charged once in a great while. Kendall couldn't wait to get back to the office with his copy of the day's offenses so that he could write and submit his portion of the copy before 4pm. That was his deadline the editor set for him. He had free rein to write about whatever new charges on the blotter he wanted as long as he included all the ones on the list that were felonies. He could skip the bullshit misdemeanors and the editor would have removed most of them anyway because there was only so much room on the paper for his section. He also had reign, within his time constraints, to do any research and follow ups on the cases he published as long as they fit into his allotted section on the print and were turned in on time.

He had an inside tip at the police station with one of the guards that worked the jail side of the street. He decided to juice this one up for some more information on this case. A quick stop across the street at the jail might buy him enough information to include a good write up for this rare bit of news.

Kendall met with his informant and got all the juice he needed to include a solid report. Apparently, Lamar Jackson, aged 26, was a repeat offender and decided on this particular evening, to steal a woman's purse in the witness of the rest of his posse. When the lady resisted, he used a disproportionate amount of force and essentially kicked the woman into submission all the while breaking an arm, her neck, and some ribs. The report suggested that a few of her ribs had punctured her lungs and she was in the ICU at Mercy Hospital. He figured this was about as juicy a bit he was going to be able to offer today and headed back to the office to write off his copy.

<h1 style="text-align:center">X</h1>

Garrett sat down to breakfast and was planning a walk around the harbor when he finished. He glanced over his plate of eggs at the folded paper he got while out for his morning constitution around the park down the street. Something drew him straight to the police blotter. He scanned the usual suspects and came across something that horrified him and brought that all too familiar twinge to the surface of his skin. The one that raises all the hairs and makes you feel like there is someone watching you. Of course, there wasn't, but the feelings were legitimate and he focused on one line in particular that caught his attention. Lamar Jenkins, aged 26, arrested and bonded out on charges of attempted murder and theft of a purse on an 82 year old Druid Hill resident.

This was the one he was looking for. His next project. He committed to spending the next couple of days or so looking into this incident and learning all he could about the victim and the scumbag Lamar. He got that same feeling every time his unit went into the bush for another mission. He knew he wasn't going to get much sleep over the next couple of days so he threw his cold eggs into the trash, set the plate into the sink, and headed out the front door on his own personal mission.

First stop was the police station, to get a copy of the police report on Lamar Jenkins. It was amazing how much information is available to the public with a bit of knowledge about the Freedom of Information Act. At a small cost, he was able to get the full report. Court papers are usually pretty thorough because a case has to be won on its merits and content. All the t's crossed and i's dotted. Garrett did some more research and found an address for Lamar as well as one for Hazel. He decided to take a trip to the hospital and check on Hazel and get some more details about the assault.

Hazel was still in the ICU under heavy sedation to keep her pain under control; also so she doesn't try to rip out her tubes. Garrett wasn't allowed to see her but he met with one of the neighbors in the waiting room. He lied and said that he met her a few years ago at a church retreat and heard about her trouble. He got more details about the incident that put her there and was aghast at the details of her injuries. He had a name and it was burning a hole in his brain. Lamar Jenkins...LAMAR "the monster" JENKINS. He started getting a headache just thinking about it.

He flashed back to one mission in the jungle that had him rattled. He hadn't thought about it since he got back to the states but he knew it would carry with him forever. He was in a remote mountain post that his team created to watch over one of the thousands of cocaine processing labs his team was responsible for dismantling. In this particular lab, the cartel were using children from the local village as watchdogs. They were each issued a Kalashnikov; What we know as an AK 47. Only these were Chinese knockoffs. The prices were cheaper and more readily available than their soviet counterparts. Garrett's detail was given the green light to take the lab out. His personal objective in this mission was the elimination of all security details. It happened that on the night they were going to attack, there were several children standing guard. Garrett, against his conscious, took all three out, silently, with his tactical knife. He remembered grabbing each one of their mouths with one hand and inserting the knife into the base of their skulls.

The initial insertion was just like butter but there is an odd crunch as the tip of the blade enters the gap between the first vertebra and the orifice at the base of the skull. It is an upward like movement and Garrett was taught to add a twist of the blade to ensure complete severance of the spinal cord. The result is usually immediate death but two of the children were still moving their mouths, gasping for their last breath, and looking at him with their thousand yard stares. This really stuck with Garrett for the rest of his time in the jungle. He didn't think much about it since then, until now. Something about this Lamar Jenkins triggered this memory and he didn't really understand why but now he was stuck with those memories in his head.

Lamar lived in a neighborhood near Druid Hill Park. It was his mother's house and as he surveilled the address from a bench at the park, he realized that it was populated with children. He had to come up with a plan to nab this mush brain somewhere away from the house. Since he wasn't on house arrest or wearing a monitoring device, he was free to roam the hood with his compatriots. It didn't take long for Garrett to see him coming out of his mother's house with another numskull. He followed them to a corner store where they were buying cigarettes and a couple of 40s. After another block and a half, they stopped at a vacant lot near an overpass.

There was a larger group of people there listening to a boom box that was blaring some kind of hip hop. Garrett didn't understand the gang banging mentality of the music. He believed it was so influential to these people that there had to be some responsibility for the way the world was turning out. At least this little part of the world anyway. He was so disgusted with it, he started to feel sick to his stomach.

He was used to having stress induced sick spells while in the bush. Most of the training that he had was so brutally physical that he learned how to throw up and run at the same time. It was almost a right of passage to be on a 12 mile ruck march and not throw up at least a couple of times. He hunched over and relieved himself and continued to evaluate the situation for any weaknesses where he could slip in and snatch Lamar. The way the group interacted seemed like it would be too much of a risk trying to take him while they were together. What could he do to separate him from the herd? He wanted to take some time to think about it and headed back to his car. He felt comfortable enough to leave the area for now as he would know, generally, where to find him.

Back at his apartment, Garrett was formulating a plan on how to debilitate Lamar, with the most efficiency, without killing him. Something he recalled on TV a while back was about an industrial accident that happened at a metal fabrication shop. A man was using a big metal brake to bend a piece of steel plate.

The machine is basically two, long, heat treated dies that are attached to a base and moveable upper jaw. Something like a giant mouth. Except on this one, the bottom jaw, or die in this case, is stationary and the upper die moves up and down. A cross section of the dies would show the bottom die looked like it was shaped like a hollow U shape and the top die was like a solid U shape that fit perfectly into the bottom. When a piece of metal is placed between them and lowered together, the metal gets pushed in a straight line down into the lower U shaped die and causes the ends to bend upward. Depending on how far down you bring the top die will determine the degree or angle of the bent metal. These dies can be anywhere from a couple of feet long to 20 feet long.

The power they exert on a downward movement can be tens of tons depending on how thick the metal is that needs to be bent. In the news incident, the operator of the brake was adjusting the piece of steel that he was trying to bend when his foot slipped on the actuator pedal and the top die came down, pinching his hand between the piece of steel and the top die. It crushed his hand to the point of severing it off right in the middle of his palm. The crushing action actually pinched of all of the major vessels so there was very little bleeding.

This report that he saw on TV gave him an idea for how he was going to maim this scumbag. Where in the world was he going to find a brake? Maybe he could head over to the old Bethlehem Steel Shipyard and see if there are any around at night that he could use. He would scope that out in a day or two. In the meantime, he decided because this poor woman was kicked to within an inch of her life, he was going to remove his feet. A life altering debilitation that this piece of shit will never forget.

The shoreline of Chesapeake Bay is littered with various boat yards, factories, but one of the most iconic sites is the Bethlehem Steel Works and Shipyard. Not far from Essex along the 695 corridor, you can't miss the massive chimneys and gantry cranes that house the blast furnaces and mill houses. Dating back to at least World War 2, this shipyard has been involved in the manufacture of good American steel and ships that have been all around the world. The shipyard closed down most of its operations years ago and the steel mill wasn't doing very good financially either.

The economy was in a recession and the demand for US steel was competing with the cheaper and better Japanese and Chinese companies. Most of the sheds at the shipyard were abandoned and had been for years. Garrett was able to find a way through the fence and during the late twilight hours he made his way around the old yard. Dumpsters full of scrap steel and abandoned bicycles were a common site. Bicycles were used all over the yard for transportation from one end to the other, for efficiency. Golf carts weren't that prevalent during its heyday and most of the workers could easily procure a bike to get the mile from one end to the other. It was a convenient way to get tools and supplies to the graving docks where the ships were built or repaired.

Garrett was looking for the metal shop. He did some research online and found an old map that detailed some of the shops that were present when the yard was in its boom period. The metal shop was just about smack dab in the middle and he found a door that was ajar. The faded blue paint of the metal sheeting covering the walls reminded him of some of the pieced together cocaine labs that he blew up in Colombia. As he entered the shop he didn't realize the immensity of the space. The ceiling appeared to be at least 25 feet tall and the machinery was enormous.

After some looking around, he found a small metal brake that looked like it hadn't been used in years. *I guess not, its been closed for quite a while now*, he said to himself. Next, he checked to see if it was operable. It appeared to have all of its parts. This was important because there was news of thefts by scrappers and parts thieves when the place closed down. He searched for the power button and found it off to the side. When he pressed the green, on button, nothing happened. *SHIT! No power.* "There has to be a breaker box around here somewhere!" He scanned the room. Way in the back he spotted a few large grey boxes that appeared to be breakers. *The electricity has to be on*, he thought. *The masthead lights are on outside. I guess to deter any would be mischief.* He approached one of the boxes and was just able to make out some of the writing on the lid. He looked for the brake slot and found one in the second box over. He flipped it to the on position and went back over to the brake. He hit the green button and heard the motor start to rev up. "YESSSS!", he shouted with little care for anyone hearing.

Now Ive got this part of the plan taken care of. I'll head back and do some more thinking. I may need to take him out of here and place him somewhere he can be found. If I leave him here he won't be able to get out and probably won't be found. There was a night patrol that scoured the area, once every couple of hours but they were undependable. It was assumed that the place was abandoned and to his advantage the watchmen weren't very diligent in their duties. He would need to come up with an ending to this performance, so he made his way to the hole in the fencing and back to his car.

The air that evening was thick with humidity. It was one of those nights that made you wet without touching any water. All the hiking around the shipyard and skulking around the fence line was giving him a case of "swamp ass". Wearing jeans didn't help the matter;

they didn't breathe like sports pants and those made from polyester blends. He wasn't a stranger to this affliction. He got it so often in the jungles of Colombia he got into the habit of bringing diaper cream with him in his rucksack. Turned out he wasn't the only one that needed it out in the bush so he included several tubes in his med kit.

During his jungle training in Hawaii, one of his instructors was a veteran of the Vietnam War. He explained how patrols started going "commando" just to avoid the friction of wet underwear. Apparently, not including underwear worked quite well. The newer materials used to manufacture the BDUs, coupled with the rash cream were God sends when there wasn't a way to take a bath for days or weeks. Wipes had also come a long way and several companies developed wipes specifically for field operations. Little ridges and adding aloe, etc...were all technologies that tried to ease this horrible nuisance. Its not easy to keep clean when you are sitting in a hole for days at a time. Garrett thought back at how funny it was that he never smelled bad to himself and never really noticed any of his team smelling bad. He giggled thinking that they must have just gotten used to it and it didn't bother them anymore. Coming back to the command post and taking a shower was such a relief and if any of them did catch a bad case of "The Ass" it sometimes took a week to clear it up.

Being in a constantly wet environment has its challenges, especially for a medic. Infections can grow and spread exponentially and there is a constant threat of "trench foot" if socks aren't changed regularly. This problem could end a mission for an individual almost single-handedly. It is kind of like when you have been in the pool too long and your hands start to wrinkle. Well the same thing can happen to your feet when they are wet for extended periods of time and constrained by socks and boots. Even the best hot weather or jungle boots still don't have the drying capabilities to beat the humid and wet conditions of the jungle. Losing the ability to walk can be a death sentence in that environment.

In training, they basically had two sets of everything. One they wore during the day when they were trekking around and setting up camp for the evening. Then they would change into the dry gear for their rest and sleep times. They hung their wet gear out and just wound up having to put them back on wet the next day. Psychologically, it takes a special kind of person to be tolerant of that type of environment and still be able to perform at the top of their abilities. Garrett was one of those people and was fortunate not to be laid out with anything major that would have sidelined him from the missions. Working smart in that environment is the only way to survive it and come back whole.

When he arrived back at his apartment he went right into the shower to clean off the build up of salts and slime that he felt. He paid special attention to the crack of his ass and the inner thighs between his legs and scrotum. This is where problems arise, up to and including fungal infections, if not treated properly. A case of jock itch was not in his future if he could help it. Just for added measure, when he got out, he put on some of the diaper creme. The hot spots between his legs were an indication that jeans might not be the best attire for this mission going forward.

He spent the rest of the evening trying to figure out what to do with Lamar after he removed his feet. There were some shady neighborhoods not far away in Essex that he was going to look at the next day. If he stays near the river he might be lucky enough to find an abandoned house that he can drop him off at. At the worst he thought he could drop him in one of the alleys that run through the main street of Essex. He would definitely be found in one of those places. Essex, not unlike most of the neighborhoods that are close to the city, has its areas that are infected with homeless and drug addiction. He would certainly find something close to the shipyard where he could ensure that Lamar would be found. Much like his views with Scott, he wanted Lamar to suffer for this with a memory that would never leave him until the day he died. Garrett just didn't want that to be too soon because he wanted him to fully suffer for his sins.

He justified his thoughts and actions by considering the level of evil he was battling. Just like he thought he was battling pure evil in the jungle. Those monsters were preying on people who were weak and couldn't avoid the addiction to their product. Those people sure as shit didn't care about the trails of carnage they left behind in people's shattered lives. Knowing that one simple thing cleared Garrett's conscious almost immediately. Yes, he was leaving is own level of carnage behind him when they destroyed these labs but he surmised that his battle was the more honorable one. He felt like a protector of humankind, a sort of wielder of the scepter of good. He thought he remembered somewhere in the bible about the necessity of battling evil. He reflected on stories of wars being fought for good all throughout the old testament. Entire cities would fall at the glory of the righteous. The more he told himself these things, the better he slept at night. In his mind, he was God's hands here on earth. Doing the good and bringing light back into the darkness. It isn't easy to clear a conscious when it starts out with doubts. He starts his out with nothing but positive and assured righteousness.

The morning brought with it a renewed energy for this mission. He started out for Essex. Within a half hour of riding around, He found an old truck that he could boost nearby and thought that would be best so he could drop it back off when he was done. It was in the parking lot of an abandoned Kmart.

Using the same methods he used before, he determined that it was a good option and didn't appear to be used in quite some time. He started it and it had plenty of gas to get the job done. The bed of the truck was big enough to put him in and cover with a tarp. It would be perfect for transportation, which was its only purpose in this mission.

Now that he had the transportation and means of removal figured out, he just needed to shadow Lamar for a week or so to determine an exact plan for extraction. He needed to find a small window when he was alone, outside, and vulnerable. That turned out to be more of a problem for him than he originally thought. Lamar was constantly with someone either drinking or walking around the neighborhood. His mother's house was out of the question because someone was always there. No, he figured he was going to have to do something a bit more creative. Perhaps posing as someone that wants to buy some drugs would work the best. It was going to be a snatch and grab. He noticed a particular lot that he and his friends frequented, especially on weeknights, where they would sell drugs, party, and listen to loud music. The key to this part of the operation was going to be a diversion. The loud hip hop music seemed like a good cover. He would approach Lamar in the truck and act like he wanted to buy some drugs. He figured he might be armed and he would have to act fast with the chloroform. Since he wasn't wearing a shirt, usually, he would have to figure out how to hold him so he wasn't going to slip away with all the sweat from the weather they were having. He planned it out to the last detail and decided to strike next Wednesday evening.

Wednesday...Hump Day...Why is it always on a Wednesday? That was a good middle of the week day and the cops were not a frequent scene in this part of town. He only had to worry about the gang of people he would be with. The lot where they hung out was under an overpass. There were some retaining walls directly adjacent to the empty grass lot and if he was parked at just the right angle, which he could control by parking there, he would avoid the larger crowd and maybe only have to deal with one other person. He might have to shoot them in the leg or something just to paralyze them for the moment while he worked on Lamar. He did a dry run by driving by the site one morning when no one was there. He got out and checked all the angles and felt comfortable that this plan was the best option. Wednesday was going to be the day that Lamar's life would change forever.

XI

Wednesday, 2130p, Essex, abandoned Kmart parking lot.

Garrett didn't take more than 5 minutes to hot-wire the truck and started making his way to Druid Hill. It was just about in the northern middle of the city so he was looking at about a 20-25 minute drive as long as the traffic was fair. He checked his bag to make sure he had everything: Gun; check, Chloroform; check. "Good to go boy!", he screamed to himself. *We gonna catch us a black monster and it ain't gonna come easy.* He hadn't gotten the same rush this time as he did on the last one. He figured it was just the way he was settling in to this new way of approaching his new life as a civilian. He was channeling all of his energy into the details and wasn't worried so much in the outcome. *WORK THE PLAN STAN! Just work the plan.*

This was also the mentality of his training. Make a plan and stick to it. The fluidity only needs to be exercised if something goes wrong during the execution. Often, while in the jungle, he had to become agile during an operation. A slight miscalculation in the number of guards and the entire plan would take another trajectory. Usually, once the bullets start flying there is an air of chaos that ensues on the untrained person. Fight or flight kicks in and without a solid background, it usually leads to flight. He pictured all of those workers running for their lives as he sprayed 5.56mm bullets into everything in his line of sight. That type of saturation was more for show than effect and he knew that. Strike enough fear into the group and they will run for the hills. *Run to the Hills, Run for Your LIIIIFFFEEE!* he sang to himself. That memory reminded him of the song by Iron Maiden. *Keep your mind on one thing you idiot. Your about to go into battle so stay focused, man!*

He realized he missed the turn with all that floating around in his head and had to make a u-turn. As he did, he noticed one of Baltimore City's finest parked up the top of the hill. His stomach sank for a moment as he raced to make up a backstory about the truck. He was sure the license plate was still good. He would just say he borrowed the truck from a friend so he could help somebody move. But what was the address? He was excellent on the fly and figured he would just blurt whatever number came to his mind. Clinton street he remembered from the address for Hazel's house. He would use that and the cop probably wouldn't even think about the number. He would have to take his chances.With a sigh of relief he was looking in the rear view mirror and the prowler was still parked in the same spot. Son of a bitch was probably taking a nap. It was around 1000pm and they probably got done eating their supper and decided to pull off to take a little snooze before shift change at 1100.

Garrett pulled towards the empty lot and decided to take a drive by and make sure everything was in place. As he passed the lot, he took an estimated head count. He also spotted Lamar in the crowd with his 40 ounce gripped in his worthless, piece of shit hand. By the looks of it, it was a colt 45; not as tasty as a Micky's but packs the same kind of punch. He giggled to himself thinking about how relaxed Lamar would be with a couple 40s in him. He won't know what hit him when he gets that first inhalation of chloroform. As he passed the lot he drove a little slower to double check the angle of attack. Everything was looking like a go. He went under the underpass and went around the block to make his final approach. As he pulled up he shouted, "Yo bro! lookin for some goodies!"

"Yo nigga, what u say? U lookin for some goodies?" It was the guy standing next to Lamar. He looked over at Lamar and said, "Yo homie, check whitey out! He lookin fo sum goodies!" The whole group started laughing.

"Yeah man! I lookin fo some goodies, got some fo me?" Lamar took a long look at Garrett and told him to pull up at the corner. This was the moment Garrett knew his plan was going to move forward with absolute success. He reached over and grabbed his Glock 22. He had the 40 caliber locked and loaded just in case. He reached over and grabbed the chloroformed rag and got out of the truck as Lamar was approaching him. As luck would have it, he was alone! Garrett couldn't believe it. How in the world could this kind of luck follow him around. A quick look again and he decided to act. He slipped the Sig into his back belt and stepped all the way out of the truck. "What u lookin for nig......." and that was all he got out before Garrett grabbed the back of his neck and shoved the rag over his mouth and nose. He did it so quick and hard that he felt his nose crack in his hand.

That one swift move had Lamar's legs wobbling and eyes rolling till you could see the bright whites. Garrett, acting as quickly as he could, grabbed Lamar by the belt loop and bending his legs, heaved him up and over the bed of the truck. He snapped back into the open drivers door. He purposely left the truck running and slammed it into drive. In his mind the entire operation was less than 10 seconds. He sped off yelling a loud "YAHOO!" He was so damn proud of himself for the smooth way it went down. He took a quick look through the back window as Lamar lay there with his arms and legs akimbo. Unconscious and unaware of what was coming next! He drove back around, making his way to 695 and to the shipyard. He held up his hand and gave the middle finger to the cops that were still parked in the same spot, just for good measure. They were, obviously, sleeping. Any act of aggression like a finger to the face, would have spawned an all out pursuit. Garrett knew better. He gave the truck some gas and headed down the road.

When he arrived at the abandoned shipyard, he did a quick visual sweep from the top of the hill to make sure there weren't any security guards roaming around. To his relief, as expected, there wasn't a soul in sight. He took Lamar out of the bed and threw him over his shoulder.

Walking with another adult human on your shoulder is no easy feat. Especially trying to traverse down a hill. Garrett finally relented to the awkwardness of it and decided he wasn't going to do any harm. He decided to roll him down the hill. Lamar wound up crashing into the fence hard enough to make a hell of a racket. Garrett quickly followed after him and drug him to the hole he hid in the fence. After wiggling him through and putting him back on his shoulder he trudged to the metal shop.

There was a rolling, targeting table he placed him on. It was used to weld plate and bar onto when setting up targets for the pipe fitters. The table was about 6 x 15 feet and had casters so it could be moved around the shop. He unlocked the casters and rolled the table, feet first, over to the metal brake that he already set up the other night. He never turned the breaker back. He hit the green button and heard the machine start right up. Using the foot actuator, he got the dies as far apart as he could and started sliding Lamar's feet between them. He figured the ankles were as good a place as any to pop his feet off. With a devious smile, he mashed on the foot pedal. As the dies came down and touched his ankles, the machine didn't even moan, as if it was under a load. It just kept on going down and as it did, Lamar let out a loud, ear-piercing scream.

Garrett lost the tepid flush to his face as he scrambled to put his hand over the mouth of that vile creature. He left the dies in the down position and reached in his pocket for the chloroform soaked rag. He quickly removed his hand over Lamar's mouth and placed the wet rag there. His tongue was fighting to push the rag back out of his open mouth. Unfortunately, the tongue just doesn't have the advantage here. Lamar's tear soaked eyes rolled back into his head again and the rest of his body went limp. Garrett peeked over at the creature's legs and took a walk around to the back of the machine. The several tons of force had already done their job. The back of the dies looked exactly as Garrett expected. Small lines of blood where the feet would be but, other than that, just metal dies.

The feet were lying on the dirty concrete floor with just a small puddle of blood around each one. One was lying on its side, no white bones to see, just a crimped edge with some blood leaking through. The other foot was a couple of feet away and standing straight up as if it was still attached to Lamar's standing body. This gave Garrett a little chill to think that just a moment ago they were attached to someone. It appeared that there was just that bit of blood loss and he walked back around to the front of the brake. He mashed the actuator and lifted the top die about 8 inches. The ends of the legs were completely flat. Literally crimped with almost no blood except what was pooled in the bottom of the die. Crimped just like the feet in the back. He sat there for a minute and took in the moment. He was flashing to a particularly brutal battle scene he remembers where they used grenades to breech one of the labs. There were body parts everywhere. He didn't have any feelings about the subject, in particular. Just the vision of all the body parts and the lack of an equivalent of blood. Bomb trauma, just like grenades, tend to lessen the immediate blood loss because of pressure. The blast produces pressure waves and a lot of the damage can be internal. The friction of high moving shrapnel, through the air, can cause the metal fragments to heat up, helping to cauterize the wound as it enters the body. It didn't stop the blood loss but it certainly minimized the appearance in Garrett's mind. He was absolutely amazed at how well that worked. He didn't have to use a torch to cauterize the ends. *This is my best idea yet*, he thought to himself.

Garrett grabbed Lamar's shoulders and drug what was left of him all the way onto the table. He wheeled it to the center of the shop. He reached into the job bag and got out the branding iron and torch.

While he was heating it up, cherry red, Lamar started to stir a little. Garrett had to reapply the chloroform. It had the usual eye rolling effect and sent the shithead back into dreamland. When the metal of the brand was screaming back at him, he rolled Lamar onto his stomach and placed the red hot metal directly on his back, between the shoulders, just like Scott Finlay.

The sizzle of the skin and immediate smell of burnt flesh and hair punched Garrett right in the nose. He was off to the side of the table and felt like the escaping steam from the site went directly up his nostrils. He rubbed his nose on his sleeve and was determined to wear a mask, or at least a bandanna, the next time, if ever, he had to do that again. He then grabbed a roll of gauze from the inside pocket of his bag and went to work bandaging each of the flat stumps the best he could. This wasn't a combat operation and he had zero sympathy for this scumbag. He was doing this just to keep any dirt out. He wanted this piece of shit to live a long, miserable life, thinking about every person he hurt, traumatized, and tortured. This was the first day of the rest of Lamar's miserable life on this planet and Garrett couldn't be happier. He made his way out of the shop smiling all the way and thinking about the intense pain he was going to be in when he finally woke up. He would be screaming so loud there would be no way those roaming security guards wouldn't hear him.

Garrett slipped through the fence and climbed the hill, started the truck and drove off, back to the empty lot at the Kmart.

XII

Detective Sergeant Paul Young was sitting at his cubicle working on some neglected reports that he needed to file before he went home for the evening. He heard the phone ringing on Detective Dower's desk. She was in the copy room making up some mugshot sheets for another case they were working on when she heard the phone ringing. She ran out just in time to pick up and on the other end of the line was the duty sergeant for the eastern district. Apparently the Baltimore County police wanted her to come take a look at a crime scene out at the Bethlehem Steel Works. She got the details, hung up the phone, and went right over to Paul's desk. Her look was all he needed to know that he wasn't going home anytime soon. "Hey Cel, ya know I can tell we in for a long one. Wadda ya say we stop for somthin to eat?"

"Sure Paul, lez stop at Captain James'. I been dreamin bout them skrimps for a couple weeks."

"You know it! Lemme git my coat. You payin do! I ain't got it like dat!"

"I got ya big boy! You get da nest one, Deal?" With that they headed out through the city to Boston Street.

When they arrived at the abandoned shipyard, they were met at the gate by one of the Baltimore County detectives. Richard Kepler was a 20 year veteran of the force and did a few tours in Iraq during the earlier operations. *He a tall SOB,* Paul thought. His neatly trimmed mustache and expensive suit made Paul a little jealous. *Maybe dey pay dem a little more out here in de county.* Richard introduced himself and gave them a quick briefing on the findings. He indicated that the victim was on his way to University of Maryland Shock Trauma Center. He was stable enough not to need a life flight but wasn't going to walk again for a long time, if ever. When he described the gruesome amputation, both Paul and Cecilia cringed. They really dropped their jaws when they saw the machine the suspect used to do the job. They all entered the machine shop and saw little if any blood. Detective Kepler walked them over to the brake machine. "This was what the suspect used to amputate both of his feet."

"Well where are they, detective?" said Cecilia

"Around the back here but I would make sure you get a good grip on yourself because this is going to be a bit of a shock" All three of them made their way to the back of the machine. Paul immediately started to dry heave and Cecilia let out, "Dear Gawd in Heaven! What in THE Hell!" They were all staring at the grayish brown, bloated feet, left exactly as they were by Garrett. One still in the upright position, the other laying on its side next to a small puddle of congealed blood. Both with the leg ends pinched off and flattened as though run over by a train wheel.

"I THOUGHT I SEEN IT ALL, DIS ONE DA WORST!" said Paul. He was still struggling to keep the shrimp down. It was too expensive and precious a dinner to let any of it come back up. "I think I need a moment outside!", said Cecilia. She was actually starting to tear up a little. Her level of compassion for this victim had reached the brim of the glass. It was starting to overflow as she thought of the pain and suffering this poor creature was going to feel for the rest of his life. Little did she know that he was actually a brutal thug that got what was coming to him. They both went outside the shop and collected themselves while speaking with Detective Kepler. Obtaining all the pertinent information concerning the scene: victim positioning, ancillary prop locations, scene disposition, victim statements. They made their way to their Impala and decided to get to the shock trauma unit and see if they can get any more information from Lamar.

"This has got to be da wirdist week we had in yers, huh Cel?" Paul was finally starting to collect himself after the gruesome scene they both witnessed.

"Sure seem dat way! Lez see we can't git some mo info from dis Lamar. I feel so damn sorry for dis dude! He never gonna walk agin. Don't you ever git emotional Paul? About the investigations, I mean?" She said with an air of concern in her voice. Concern for Paul's seemingly detached position, other than getting sick, on most of the gruesome details.

"Naw Cel, I try not ta think on it really. I spos I gist ain't dat kind emotional. Why you ast?"

"You my partner Paul. I mean, I cur what you think" she interposed "But I guess it good dat one us keep it together." With that they were pulling up to the University of Maryland Medical Center. They parked off to the side of the emergency room entrance, a floor down from the helipad and the trauma center. The nurse in the ER didn't have any update on the situation but directed them to the trauma center to meet with the duty nurse.

When they arrived in the trauma center they just stood there, mouths agape in amazement at the difference between the trauma unit and the regular ER. Talk about people flitting about. This was a chaotic, beautiful mess. Cecilia was, again, amazed at the organized chaos that surrounded an environment like this. Her attention was drawn to a crowd of doctors and nurses that were screaming orders back and forth for this and that: "Let's get an x-ray of the distal tib/fib times 2", "Can someone start a bolus of ringers? Make that a large bore in case this goes south!", "Where is the RT? I think we should get an ABG!" , " Darlene, please call up to OR and have a bed prepped for GS, please!". It was just a whirlwind of acronyms and directives that seemed so far above them both. Medical terminology, especially acronymic shortcuts, were the ERs language. It saved time and saved lives. An entire semester is dedicated to this art in any medical coursework. Lots of the words and phrases come from the Latin etymology but some of it is just basic english that, when put together, would only be decipherable to a medically discerning mind.

"Les see we can find someone in charge. They so damn busy hir we probly gonna have to wait." Cecilia said after she collected herself from the shock of the scene.

"Lemme see what I can do hir, Cel." Paul towered over most everyone in the room and was able to find a desk in the midst of the chaos and grabbed Cecilia's arm. They excused their way through the crowd and were able to make it over to the only desk they could find. The attendant was on the phone, presumably with the OR, explaining the current status of the patient and the need for an OR, STAT! (which in medical terms, taken from the latin "statum", means immediately). As she was setting the phone down in the receiver, Paul took the opportunity to grab what he perceived to be valuable attention, "Ma'am, I'm detective sergeant Young and this is my partner detective Dower. Do you have any status on Lamar Jenkins?"

"Sir, we are terribly busy and I don't have time to talk with you at the moment. This gentlemen just came in and is being stabilized so he can be rushed to the OR. I wish I could tell you more but you'll just have to wait in the waiting room until things quiet down (which was code for we'll get to you when we get to you!)", Darlene said with as much patience as a nurse can muster in the midst of her time sensitive duties.

"Well could you please have the doctor meet us in the waiting area when he is finished here?"

"I sure will, now you need to leave. You see there isn't enough room as it is and you are just adding to the lack of space. I'll let the doctor know when things slow down a bit. Until then I suggest you wait down the hall in the waiting area. You can't miss it, it is clearly marked." Paul took out a card and placed it in the nurse's hand before she rushed off to join the crowd of chaotic energy pulsing in and out around Lamar's gurney. "Just give that to the doc, please!"

They both decided a cup of coffee might help them prepare for the inevitable and indeterminate wait. Just as the nurse described, there was a big sign directing all of the family and friends to the waiting area down the hall. It was a quaint little area with a coffee machine and TV announcing the weather for the Baltimore area. Cecilia had been in plenty of these spaces and was trying to consider why the lighting was always dim and sparsely lit. Was it to hide the tearful mothers, fathers, and family members that occupied the space but wanted to keep their sorrows to themselves? Was it a mood thing to keep potential outbursts to a minimum? She wasn't a psychologist but liked to believe it was a little bit of both. Paul grabbed them a coffee; Cecilia's was black, just the way she wanted, and they settled down on an extremely comfortable couch to weather out the excruciating wait they faced. It could be hours before they saw anyone with direct information concerning the case. Watching the forecast helped Paul focus on something other than the obvious painful need to display patience that he was sorely lacking at most times in his life.

Almost 4 hours later, an astonishingly young man in typical green scrubs, white lab coat, stethoscope in the pocket, and blue cap on his head, entered the waiting area calling out Detective Young's name. He had his card in his hand and was scanning the room. As the detectives happened to be the only two in the room, they both stood and addressed the doctor, "Forgive me doc but I was expecting someone older!" said Cecilia with wide eyes.

" No worries, I get that all the time. My name is Dr. Padashin. I am the trauma surgeon on call this evening."

"Doc, can you tell us anything about Mr. Jenkins' condition? We are the investigating team for this case and anything you can give us would be appreciated."

"Well, let me first start by saying that this is a most unusual case for me. A double amputation at the lower tib/fib region. I have only seen this once before in a train accident. Usually the patient, in a drug or alcohol induced state, trips or falls asleep on the train tracks and when a train goes by, SHWOOOP! off come the feet, legs, or whatever happens to be across the tracks at the time. Considering what information I was given about the injuries, I was shocked, to say the least. This man was found in an abandoned metal shop, on a table, with both of his feet severed off. Is that accurate?"

"Yes sir, that is what we have been told. One of the roving security guards came across him wailing in pain. You can imagine the shock when he went in and saw what he saw. The first thing he did was get sick all over the side of the table and then called for backup." Paul indicated with an almost inappropriate enthusiasm.

"What I can tell you is this is an incredibly lucky individual. The machine that severed his feet actually crushed all of the involved blood vessels and prevented him from bleeding to death before he was found. I can't even put into words the pain he must have felt. Initial blood work indicated that he had trace amounts of chloroform in his system, which would answer some questions about his state of consciousness during the amputation. Chloroform isn't really used any more for anesthesia because of the side effects it causes. It might explain the shaking and shivering he was experiencing when he was brought into the trauma center."

"Chloroform, huh?" Cecilia reacted with a Holmesian inquisitiveness. She made a mental note to check the files on Scott Finlay to see if there was a correlation with the use of this in his case.

"Yes ma'am, as I said, it was used up to about the middle of the 20th century. It was deemed obsolete for use as a general anesthetic with the advent of drugs like Halothane and Sodium Pentothal. Anyway, I had to remove about 4 inches of the lower legs because of the compression trauma. After about 3 hours on the table I was able to clean the ends up and close him. He will be sedated for quite a while during the next few weeks and will probably endure months and months of therapy just to be able to use what's left of his limbs. It is sufficed to say that he just had a complete life changing incident and will be suffering with it for a very long time."

"Will we be able to speak with him soon, Doc?"

"I would say come back tomorrow, later in the day because I have induced a coma to help him ease out of the trauma. He probably won't be able to speak, at a minimum, until then. One last thing, detectives. There was a very distinct brand on Mr. Jenkins' lower back. I couldn't really make it out but we took a picture of it for his files. It was a recent burn in because the edges hadn't started healing yet. It wasn't deep enough to warrant debridement but we did put some medicine on it to avoid any unwanted infections. I have given the nurses a standing order to make sure he is rolled back and forth from side to side every couple of hours to ensure he isn't on his back until it has healed."

"Thank you for that information doctor. *I'm gonna check the other file for these points of interest and check if there is any overlap*, she said to herself. Well shit! I guess it is what it is. Thank you very much doctor. We will be in touch if we have any more questions pertaining to the injuries. Come on Paul, time to go home and get some rest. We got some work to do tomorrow!" With that final word, Cecilia was on her way out into the hall with a pace that indicated a modicum of frustration. Paul had seen it before and couldn't help but sympathize as he wanted to get out of there hours ago. When they got out of earshot, Cecilia, with an unlikely enthusiasm whispered to Paul, " First thing mañana, I wanna look over de file on Scott Finley and see what connection dere is to chloroform and dis brand. I ain't recall either stickin out at me durin de vestigation but somethin tellin me dere a link."

"Sound like you got a hunch, Cel. You think dey might be connected?"

"Well dat two very odd cases in a couple weeks that stand out from de usual assaults and battery cases we see. It be interestin if dere was any bloodwork to show dis. We may be onto somethin. You get a chance to see if we have any background on dis Lamar Jenkins? It would really be interestin if he had a criminal record, like we found with Mr. Finlay."

"Alright Cel, I'll get on it first thing in the mornin. Jus need to go home and get some rest. I feel like this waitin was a complete waste of time!"

"I disagree, dis thing with de chloroform was a lead on somethin, I am sure. Anyway, get me back to my car so I can go home and get some sleep. I want to be ready for tomorrow. Fresh, you know?" They got out into the parking lot, back to the sounds of the city and the chaos of a 24/7 trauma center. Paul leaned back in the driver's seat and looked forward to getting home and grabbing a beer to unwind after the day he just went through.

On the other side of the city, downtown, at the Baltimore Sun offices on St. Paul Street, Kendall Firth was busy at work copywriting for the next edition of the police blotter. He was going through some of his files and came across the notes he took a couple weeks ago. They were concerning an article his colleague wrote, about a man found with all of his fingers amputated from his hands. He was found in Pigtown and the circumstances surrounding the incident weren't completely clear. There were, currently, no suspects in custody. This struck a nerve with him, when he read it, being the curious type of reporter. The reason it grabbed his attention was another article he read in a competing paper, concerning Lamar

Jackson being found at the Bethlehem Steel Shipyard with both of his feet amputated.

He recalled the name from a recent blotter he wrote, that included a case for the brutal assault and battery of an older woman in the Druid Hill neighborhood. His immediate reaction, as with any light bulb moment, was one of excitement and intrigue. He wanted to explore the idea that the crimes were connected. He just needed to find someone close with the cases that can help him with his research. He decided not to tell anyone at the paper until he finished his investigation. This was going to be the story that would get him a Pulitzer!

It has to be connected and you have to write an amazing article first. FIRST! You can't share this with anyone until you are sure, he was thinking. *You don't need anyone's help at the paper anyway. If anyone catches wind of this here, they will discount my work as that of a second rate reporter. I have been working at this damn blotter for a year now and haven't been given any real opportunities,* he said to himself. Being a graduate of University of Maryland's journalism program, he thought he might have moved up the ranks at the paper by now; at least gotten a full time reporters job. This was his ticket to be punched and he wasn't going to let anyone get in the way of that.

XIII

In a quaint, smoke free, double room, between a blue, polka dotted comforter, and 700 thread count sheets, lie Trish Kantwell and her current lover, Tom Petersen. The smell of freshly made love permeated the room and the rapid breathing indicated just exactly how fresh that session was. She was cuddled up to him with her leg straddling his, her hand playing with the one or two hairs on the space between his well defined pectoral muscles. Just below the hair was the faintest puddle of sweat forming as a result of the coital bliss. She reached down between his legs to his still, semi-erect penis and gave it a gentle massage. "If you keep that up, it's going to get hard again and you know what that means. The only way to make it go away is to have a go again. Are you up for that kind of punishment?"

"Not really but what I am ready for is a shower. Care to join?" She looked at him with that seductive grin that made all of her suitors turn into a kind of knee knocking, slobbering idiot. Tom was different. Her looks and innuendos didn't affect him the same way. The fact that he was "happily" married might have something to do with that. He watched as she extricated herself from the oddly comfortable hotel bed, slender body and perfect heart-shaped ass. She was a 9 for looks. He couldn't take his eyes off that perfectly curved ass. His idea of the perfect naked woman had to include that. He heard the shower start and the glass doors close. That glimpse of her got him aroused again and he reached down and gave it a couple strokes. He was always amazed at his ability for a quick turnaround after a good snogging. His imagination took hold and he spent another 3 minutes working his rod to a second eruption.

Tom was a hard working man and loved his family. Lately his wife had been distant both in conversation and in the bedroom. He never cheated before but when he met Trish, his whole moral compass seemed togo right out the window. Isn't that how it always happens? The real ones that suffer are the children. He tried not to think about them in the same brain space he used for his conjugal visits with Trish. This particular tryst had some particular meaning for him. It had been a couple of months since he started seeing Trish and he was starting to have "feelings" outside of the usual ones like lust. He felt more passion and romance. He felt compelled to treat her to roses and fancy dinners. He wanted to spend more time with her than he was able. It was very much like falling in love in the usual manner but he was living this dual life.

He was pretty sure his wife didn't suspect anything because his alibi always incorporated work. He didn't meet Trish during the evenings. It was only when he could slip away from the office for a long lunch. Trish seemed to be OK with the arrangement and didn't push him for more. As a matter of fact, for Trish, it was more about the sport. She enjoyed the cat and mouse games and went out of her way to seduce and retreat several times before even allowing the first encounter. This was her modus operandi.

Tom woke up from a power nap after his second ejaculatory high to hear the whir of the hair dryer in the bathroom. *I couldn't have been out that long, she is still in the bathroom*, he convinced himself. When she opened the door, standing there with her arm leaning against the doorjamb like a Humphrey Bogart leading lady, smoking a cigarette, all he could think about was how it was all going to end. Was he going to break it of with his wife of 22 years and leave the kids with the burden of 2 holiday schedules? Was Trish going to eventually get bored and dump him for the next exciting chase? He hadn't thought this way until that switch went off inside that went from casual to all out obsession. "When I left you to take a shower, you had that rabbit in the fox's den look on your face. Now I see and smell a hint of apprehension and perhaps a tinge of fear...What is it darling?", she added to the leading lady allure.

"I was just thinking about us and where it goes from here. I guess I hadn't really spent any time pondering it. Does it bother you that I am having these thoughts?" he tried to reassure her.

"Not at all, in honesty, I was wondering when this conversation was going to come up. You know that I don't spend my time dwelling on things and I certainly would be the first to say not to ruin a good thing but....." she hesitated so that she could choose her words carefully, "Well, I think I am starting to have stronger feelings for you than I originally thought."

"Well isn't that ironic. I didn't take you for the type. Just kidding, I know we are all human and feelings change like the wind. Blowing one way in the favor of a downwind run and dead ahead on a luff the next. I still haven't said anything to my wife and, frankly, wouldn't know where to start. I, obviously, care very deeply about you after the last couple of months but I also care very deeply about my children. I don't want to see this turn into an amateur boxing match with a courtroom as the ring."

"I'm going to leave it in your good hands to figure it out but remember, I am here too and I don't like sharing." That last phrase took a dark turn in Tom's mind. For some reason, his subconscious was taking over and flooding his thoughts with all kinds of devious and scary scenarios. If there is one thing he certainly doesn't need, it is a long drawn out divorce over an adulterous adventure in the midst of a marital stagnation.

Trish was getting dressed and as he watched he decided to table his feelings the best he could and devote some time in the near future to planning what is best for all parties involved. On the one hand, he knew that Trish was young and resilient and would bounce back from anything that happened. On the other, there was his wife that he shared a life with but didn't have the same feeling for. And on the third side of the triangle, as all great love stories involving separate lives are, were his kids. The greatest gift he was ever given, as far as he was concerned. A father would go to great lengths to protect his children. *At least most fathers*, he thought. I guess there are some real pieces of shit out there that are so self consumed, they couldn't care less what happens to their offspring. Not Tom, he wasn't going to be one of those. He just needed some time to figure things out. "Would you mind if we didn't see each other next week? I just wants some time to figure out where I go from here. I feel like I am at a crossroad and a decision has to be made that will go greatly punished if not given." he said with a sincere tone. "I hope you won't take this as a sign that I am feeling any less for you, the reality is that I am just starting to think more about them and their meaning in all of this."

"NP darling. NP. I completely understand. You do you. I will be here when you are ready to deliver your verdict.", she said with the smallest tone of contempt. There is really nothing like a woman scorned. She got the rest of her clothes on, grabbed her purse and slipped out the hotel room door. Tom laid back down on the bed, still naked, and fell back into an afternoon nap.

Kendall was leaving his office for the evening and opened his phone to a podcast from Bill Maher. He enjoyed the wit and humor but was particularly drawn to the blatant marijuana use because of the strict laws governing it here in Maryland. *Bunch of stuck up, pickle up the ass, old-timers running this state for sure*, he thought as he struggled to pay attention to the podcast. He didn't have cable TV anymore so he couldn't watch Real Time on HBO. He got his fix on the podcast, dreaming about one day being able to walk home from work with a loaded marijuana cigarette hanging out of his mouth. The best he could hope for was going to his shitty, overpriced apartment in Mount Vernon and firing up with all the windows open to keep his neighbors from calling the cops. When he got home, his sister called him, crying on the other line, "Ken, I think Tom is cheating on me!"

"What makes you think that, Kare?" Kendall said as he tried to pry himself from a ganja shrouded daydream.

"He just seems so distant lately and a few times he has been out of the office for extended lunches but no one at his work knows where he is...Am I just being paranoid? I mean, I really do sense something is wrong here! Oh my God, Ken, what am I going to tell the kids?!"

"Keep it together sis! I'll tell you what. How about if I meet Tom somewhere to have a beer or something and broach the subject with him without insinuating that you were behind the questions? Do you think that would help?"

" Please don't do that Ken, it will look to obvious. He will know I've been talking to you then."

"Well, maybe I'll follow him around for a few days to see where he goes when he leaves the office. I know times are tough and you can't hire a PI for this. He will notice the money missing and they aren't cheap anyway. The paper uses them from time to time. Hey, maybe I can ask around and see if someone might be able to help. Anyway, don't worry yourself, we'll get to the bottom of this. Until then, just act as usual and see if you can get him to come around. Goodnight Kare."

"Night little bro. Thanks again but keep it on the down low, please. I don't need him knowing about this. I really am more worried about what will happen to the kids than myself. Anyway, sleep tight." Kendall hung up the phone and blazed up a Cheech and Chong sized stick of some blue kush he bought off one of the myriad of drug dealers downtown near the office. He wondered how many of his other colleagues liked to smoke. *It is a great incentive for creativity*, he reckoned.

XIV

Garrett was home relaxing after a pizza and beer induced nap. The TV was droning in the background and like the offset path of the newtonian reflector, he had the idea to find out who was writing the blotter and see if he could sidle up for information to add to his hit list. He grabbed yesterday's paper and found the page next to the Today section. At the bottom was the name: Kendall Firth. He wondered if there was any relation to Colin Firth. *Great actor*, he thought. He would spend some time today looking for a way to contact him, inconspicuously. If he could get an inside guy then he would be able to feed his need to continue on the vigil-antic path, which needed fresh meat to fuel the burn.

This was the first time it occurred to him that he was breaking the law for doing some good in society. He was aware how broken the system was and had no remorse for being a positive cog in the wheel of justice. He played that role before in the jungles of Colombia and was just transferring that spirit into his civilian life. He looked up the Sun paper's directory and found a number for this Kendall. He dialed and waited while the chirping in the background initiated that wireless signal, sent through the air as effortlessly as a gull coasting on a thermal, which eventually reaches the other phone and is answered either in person or by a robotic voice indicating a failure to connect.

He was trying to think if there was an episode of Star Trek that might have foreshadowed this effect that we take for granted today. "The Trek", as far as Garrett was concerned, was one of the greatest predictors of technological advances the human race has ever seen. No other show has been able to display these novel ideas in their primitive forms to become what they are today. It has literally changed how the world operates. These changes, sometimes subtle and sometimes not, have effectively drawn the trajectory for the course of human civilization since they were first broadcast on TV over 60 years ago.

Garrett had took a moment, while he waited for the line to be answered, to recognize this marvel. As his mind was moving to the next thought, the other line picked up, " Hello?!" Garrett took a deep breath, collected his thoughts, refocused, and initiated, "Hi there, is this Kendall Firth I have the pleasure of speaking with?"

"Yes sir, it is. May I know who you are?" he replied almost sarcastically, as the politeness took him by surprise.

" My name is Roger. I understand you write the police blotter for the Baltimore Sun. Is that correct?"

"Yes sir. How may I help you?"

"Funny you should ask that. Is there somewhere we could meet in person? Perhaps a coffee...or something a bit stronger?" And with that, Garrett and Kendall were on their way to a symbiotic relationship that neither of them would have predicted when they woke up that morning.

Funks Democratic Coffee House in Fells Point was serving its usual crowd of about 20 people on a Thursday night. It is always open mic night on that day. Poets, small bands of musicians, and obscure Baltimore literary minds are present to provide the world with a glimpse into their latest artistic endeavors. All Kendall had to go on at the moment was a voice. He took it as an honest voice with an honest concern and he, apparently, was the key to this voice's concerns.

Garrett was scanning the room for a young man wearing a brown bombardier's jacket. That was how Kendall described to him he would look. Blonde hair and a brown bomber's jacket. He swept over to the back of the modest cafe and saw who he was looking for, ordering a large cappuccino about the size of the one from Mike Myer's character in, "So I Married an Axe Murderer". He giggled in the back of his mind at the similarities and went over to the counter to order an americano for himself. He liked his coffee black with or without one sugar depending on his mood. Tonight was a single raw sugar packet night. He would need the extra boost to encourage the neurons to keep pace with his mouth when describing to Kendall what he wanted to accomplish.

Kendall found a small corner table in the area next to the stage as a performer was engaging in a pseudo, self-immolation concerning a poem about the conflagration at the library of Alexandria, along the ancient Nile river. Garrett brought his meager americano over to the table in an arts and craft mug that they were promoting at the counter. He introduced himself as Roger and asked if it would be alright to sit down. Of course, intrigued by the hushed tones and secretive mannerisms, Kendall motioned with his hand to the chair next to him as the poet droned on in the background. "Sorry about the table but it is usually quite busy here on open mic night. So what can I do for you Roger?"

"Well Kendall, may I call you Kendall? I am looking to get a bit more information on your police blotter listings. Do you keep detailed notes of victims and investigation notes?"

" Yes you may and yes, I do keep notes of all my listings. I even keep a few inside "birdies" to get information that isn't always available to the public. Why do you ask?" Kendall was really piqued at this point.

" I am going to tell you something but it needs to stay here at this table." His foreboding figure, towering over Kendall's meek frame, seemed to take on a serious air, which caused Kendall's face to change a bit. " I spent some time during the drug wars of the 90s running around the jungles of Colombia on search and destroy missions. I want you to know that because I am not one to be trifled with and won't hesitate to end this conversation, among other things, if it goes beyond where we are now. Do you accept those terms?"

"Well sure, I guess so."

"No guessing, I need a sure yes or a sure no. *Comprende?*" He said with a staccato that reverberated across the table directly into Kendall's ears.

"Ok, yes, I understand and accept the terms. I am just not sure where you are going with this and, quite frankly, I went from curious to a bit afraid. I am glad we are here in the open."

"Well don't let that assuage your fears. Just know that I agreed to this place because of the noise and distractions. Not to mention the volume of people that help keep this conversation under the radar." Garrett was starting to relax now as he took a critical inventory of his surroundings. He wanted to be absolutely sure he would be able to control any adverse reactions to what he was about to say to this stranger.

The poet finished his oration and the crowd settled into a wild and furious round of applause and adulation. Unbeknownst to Garrett, this particular poet was a favorite of the community and drew large crowds to his performances. He leaned over to Kendall and whispered in his ear, "I have used your blotter to do some of my own work. I have taken care of some miscalculations in justice and I would like to align with you so that I may continue my work. Do you understand what I am saying?" It took a minute for Kendall to display any reaction to the words in his ear. He didn't realize that he had actually stopped breathing and was starting to see stars in his field of vision. He immediately let out his breath as the crowd settled down for the next group of performers that were taking their places on the too small stage. A drummer with a bass and snare, an acoustic guitarist and a man with a microphone. They were called "Smoke" and leaned into what sounded like folk music while Kendall tried to compose himself and articulate what he was feeling on the inside. "If I understand what you are saying, you have turned some of the names on my blotter into personal projects for the good of the community. Does that just about sum it up?"

" Without sounding too clichéd, Bingo! I have continued where the justice system has decided to cut things short. Specifically, I have taken two people from your list and ended the possibility of them being able to commit any more crimes. Something, I believe, should have been done by our justice system in the first place. Before you hyperventilate again, NO!, I did not kill them. I merely incapacitated them. I changed the trajectory of their lives to the point that they will never forget what they have done and never be able to do it again. I ensured a quality of life that would include reflection and absolute suffering until the end."

" Mr. Roger, I am at a loss of words. I am not sure I really want any more details. What I am hearing is "vigilante". Are you claiming to be a vigilante, Mr. Roger?"

"Either call me Roger or Mr. Stemway, not Mr. Roger. It sounds retarded. Are you retarded? I didn't get that impression but by all means, I am open to the idea." he interjected with a bit of sarcasm, wit, and anger.

"OK Mr. Stemway, I am sorry. You didn't give me your last name and I was trying to be respectful. So, again, how, exactly, can I help you with this?"

"Frankly, Kendall, I thought it would be obvious. You really aren't helping your case for the retarded comment. What I am asking you to do is help me get information, detailed information, that will help me to continue my work. Is the fog starting to clear now? I want you to help me narrow down, locate, and provide inside information into the crimes of people on your blotter so that I can determine if the justice system has done their part or I need to intercede on behalf of humanity. I want to be a positive contributor to a broken system. I want to help protect the better part of society from these wild animals. Let's just say that I am able to work outside the law, with boundaries that don't necessarily have limits. I want your help in finding out where they live, where they work, who they hang out with. I need these details so that I can plan to incapacitate them permanently. Now is what I am describing something you might be willing to help me with?"

The second song of the set for the band was coming to an end and the crowd, as expected, was applauding and whistling with happiness. 25 or more people hopped up on caffeine and sugar, listening to monotonous sounds emanating from an elevated stage is almost like a hypnotist's trick. When it is all over and they snap their fingers to wake up, the room comes alive. Kendall leaned over the table and his enormous empty bowl of coffee, and said, " Yes, I would like to help you." He had never been so excited and scared all at the same time. The level of emotion was 10x more than his first upside down roller coaster ride at the age of 10. At least he had his mother next to him to be an anchor for those emotions.

Here he was alone, thinking about his sister's situation, which brought ideas to the front that seemed to merge with the energy he was receiving from the stranger across the table. He felt there was an answer forming in the space between the two of them, which was going to be a unique influence to both of their lives going forward.

The two spent the next five minutes in complete silence. During the next round of applause, Garrett got up from the table and stuck out his hand. Kendall, noticing the rough, embattled appendage, returned the gesture in as tight and strong a grip as he could muster. After a single pump, Garrett released his hand and headed for the door. There were no more words exchanged between the two strangers that night but Kendall left with feelings of anxiety and excitement as he strolled down the street towards his apartment in Mount Vernon.

Days went by and Kendall hadn't heard anything from Garrett. After their conversation at the coffee house, it was all he could think about as he punched away at the keys on his laptop compiling the next blotter for the paper. Garret finally got in touch with him to see if there were any prospects. Kendall said there wasn't anything worth chasing after at the moment. It wasn't all truthful because he had an ulterior motive.

He explained the delicate situation with his sister. He asked Garrett (Roger), as an exchange of services, if he would mind trailing his brother in law to see if his sister's intuition was valid. He let him know about his sister's wish to keep Tom safe, mostly for the sake of the kids, but wanted solid evidence of any infidelity so that he could report back to his sister. Depending on the news and evidence, he assumed his sister would make a decision about continuing in the marriage or a separation. Either way, the kids were the important value in the equation. The news was either going to be positive or negative for their lives moving forward.

At almost 1100 that night, when he was starting to get ready for bed, Kendall's phone rang. It was Garrett on the other end of the line. He was outside his sister's house and Tom had just got home from work. It was a late night with drinks after work. He stayed with him all day and there wasn't anything out of the ordinary. No secret meetings, not even an escape for lunch outside of the office. There was a cafeteria on the ground floor of the building and he tracked Tom there during his lunch break. He would spend another couple of days staking it out and report back. Kendall crawled into bed that night wondering if his sister was just letting her imagination run away with her.

Miles away in the heart of the city, the lights were out in the Special Crimes Unit second floor office of the central precinct. Detectives Young and Dower had gone home for the evening. The phone rang on detective Young's desk. He left his card with the emergency room physician that day after seeing Lamar in the hospital. "Good evening detective Young, this is Dr. Padashin over at UMMC. I was looking over some case files and wanted to discuss a few variances with you. They are concerning your investigation into the feet amputation we talked about. It seems that there was a similar case over at Harbor Hospital. I am not sure you were involved in it but there was a strange admission involving the amputation of all the fingers on both hands. It turns out there are some similarities that you may find helpful to your investigation. Please give me a call back at 410-xxx-xxxx.....Have a great evening."

XV

"We bout to start dis party off!" Paul shouted to Cecilia as she was coming out of the Central Precinct back doors. The lot was full of marked cars that were waiting for their officer's to come out of roll call. "Les go before the penguins git out. Cel, hurry up! I wanna head to University Medical and check out dis Doc! What his name again, Cel?"

"I know, Im cumin! dammit! Keep yo shirt on! I told ya there might be a connection! I think his name Padawan or some fin like dat!" She was waddling as fast as her thick thighs could wiggle over to the general issue, white Impala they both shared for official business. In the sea of police cruisers, there were only two or three white Impalas that were reserved for the detectives of the various units. Unmarked with hidden lights, they were the ideal mask, for them to get around, without giving themselves away to the public.

They both wore their service pistols hidden away. Glock 22s were the current department issue. The .40 calibre packs a wallop, with 3 clips of 15 rounds. One clip was always in the weapon and 2 spares were held in separate pouches. They both had their badges on lanyards they kept hidden in their shirts. Paul always wore a suit, to ensure his jacket hid the pistol and clips on his belt. He favored his handcuffs inside the coat pocket because he felt there was already enough weight on his belt, trying to pull his pants down. "All gut and no butt will do that to a person", he used to say to Cecilia. She also wore a suit jacket when out of the office. She opted for a holster that hung from her shoulders, like Humphrey Bogart in Maltese Falcon. She wore a skirt most of the time and a belt just wasn't an option. Her purse carried her cuffs.

When they had to interview people in the neighborhood it was best to keep as much hidden as possible, because the locals didn't act kindly to police figures. Wearing common street clothing, hiding their weapons and gear, and talking in the local vernacular made them look like a pair of Jehovah's Witnesses, scouring the hood for lost souls. The Impala was new to the arsenal at the time. The hood rats were accustomed to the Crown Victorias being used for unmarked cars. When the department transitioned to Impalas, their arrest rates went up slightly. It was easier to be clandestine in a car that no one suspected. Outside of the vice squad, the Impala became the go to, unmarked vehicle. Vice was lucky because most of the vehicles they used were acquired at the impound lot. They were usually high end vehicles like BMWs and Mercedes that were taken during drug busts. Some of the vice cops rode around in cars that were bullet ridden on the side from shootouts. There were several drive by shootings a week in some of the west side neighborhoods.

Cecilia finally got into the car and they headed over to UMMC to have a chat with Dr. Padashin. They couldn't wait to hear what he found in his files that would help them with their case. When they finished with him, they were going over to Harbor Hospital and see if they could align some of the details of both cases. They would look for any clues or leads that would help them narrow down their rather wide investigative scope. If they can get some clues that lead to a motive, they might even be able to build a criminal profile. It was all a long shot but they both felt it was a positive beginning just linking two different cases from two different hospitals.

The emergency room was nothing like the day they arrived to question Lamar. It was quiet, aside from the beeping and whirring of a few machines hiding behind the flowered curtains hanging from tracks in the ceiling. There were no more than 4 patients in the space. Behind the centrally located command desk, there were what appeared to be 3 nurses talking and 2 doctors sitting opposite them in back, writing out their notes for the various cases. A beeper goes off and one of the doctors gets up to use the phone on the desk. Immediately after the page there is a voice that comes over the PA system asking for Dr. Phillips to report to radiology. Detectives Young and Dower approach the desk and break up the conversation to ask the head nurse if Dr. Padawan is available. " You mean Dr. Padashin, ma'am?" the charge nurse wanted to be sure they had the correct Dr.

"Yes ma'am" said Cecilia.

"Yes ma'am, I can page him for you. What is the nature of your visit?" With that Cecilia pulls her badge out of her shirt and flashes the credentials to the nurse. "We are here at the request of Dr. Padashin to look at a case he is working on."

"Very good ma'am. If you wouldn't mind waiting in the triage area, I would be happy to have him meet you there. It may take a few minutes because I know he stepped out to take a break. It's just down the hall through the double doors." she pointed with the same arm she cradled the phone to her chin.

"Thank you! We'll head on over there now." They both left through the automatic doors and followed the overhead signs to the triage/staging area. Cecilia led the way as Paul's attention was drawn in every direction trying to figure out the maze that is every typical hospital hallway on the planet. If it weren't for the signs, whether overhead or pasted on the wall, the average person would be lost within the first couple of minutes. A large proportion of the entranceways in a hospital are either locked or require a magnetic card to enter or leave. To their delight, the door to the triage area was neither and they opened the door and stepped in. " So this is where everyone is!" exclaimed Cecilia.

They stepped into the main filter for the emergency services department. This is where the patients make their second point of contact when they arrive in the emergency room. The nurses that man this part of the hospital are considered one of two of the greatest level of competencies, the other being those that work in the ICU. Patients, after going through the registration area, where they provide their information and insurance, after a short wait, find themselves here at the triage area. Vital systems are checked and recorded along with the complaint. If it is life threatening, this part is skipped and they are brought immediately back into the treatment area. Often they are sent back to the waiting area, for God only knows how long, until a bed is available that is commensurate with their complaint. The majority of the people they saw seated in the waiting area were leaning deeply back into their chairs napping or holding various parts of their body.

"Hey Cel, you reckon any dese people been seen in the past 3 hours?"

" I don't know Paul but I magine the wait escrutiatin! Thank God I ain't here for treatment!" She couldn't understand, as most people don't, why the ER seemed so empty and all these people were out here waiting. No sooner than she thought that, a door opened on the other side of the room and the nurse emerged, clipboard in hand, and in a loud and clear voice called out the next person on the list to be allowed into the main treatment area.

Anyone who has been there knows that it is only an invitation to move from the waiting room to the treatment area. The wait there could be another hour depending on the level and frequency of emergencies that enter the hospital. It really is a fascinating thing to watch and contemplate. This is why it is so important to put the best nurses in triage. They have to decide which cases require the more immediate attention and which do not. Just because you came into the hospital before someone else doesn't necessarily mean you will be back in the treatment area first. Paul, being the watcher that he was, was amazed at the way there was order in all the chaos. His attention refocused when he noticed Dr. Padashin emerge from yet another door adjacent to the main waiting room. The doctor scanned the area and looked directly over at both of the detectives. He motioned for them to come over so he could escort them down the halls to his office. As they crossed the room, Paul took one last look at the chaos and said a little prayer for anyone in the room that was suffering while they had to wait for help.

Dr. Padashin, a tall, lanky man of north Indian descent, shook both of their hands, "Good morning to you both. I tink you'll find vat I hab is quite interesting. Please come dis vay. It is a wery difficult to nawigate de hallways vit out a key card. Ve are on de next ploor at de udder end but der is a stap elewator down de hall dat I usually use ven I hab to come to de ER. Most ob de offices por de attending and resident doctors are on de second ploor, close to de ER. During medical school residencies, it is conwenient because dey are usually on call por 72 hours. Essentially dey lib here, in de hospital, por a couple ob days. This hospital has a dormitry next to de offices dat has bunkbeds like being in camp. (Laughing and shaking his head, as is typical with the people from India)", he explained as they traversed the maze of hallways and doors leading through the areas of the hospital the regular people don't get to see. " As I explained on de fone, I rewiewed dis particular case and der ver some interesting correlations to a case dat a colleague op mine discowered vile he vas in one ob his rewiews."

Dr. Padashin showed them both into his office. It was a relatively large office considering that it had a desk, two patient chairs opposite the desk, and a comfortable leather couch directly against the front wall. There was a glass coffee table in front of the couch and he directed them to have a seat there. He wanted to open the files out on the coffee table so they could all see. He detailed the phone call he received from Dr. Reinhold as best he remembered it:

When a case is being closed out or a patient is being transferred to another department, doctors tend to do a thorough review of the file, for both legal and administrative reasons. Each particular file has to contain all the pertinent worksheets, forms, and note pages, and be thoroughly filled out. A final review is completed, before the signed discharge form is filled out, to ensure all is in order. It is during this moment that Dr. Padashin was called by a colleague, Dr. Reinhold, over at Harbor Hospital.

He was a general surgeon, transplanted from the army field hospitals in Iraq. He performed lots of surgeries on bomb victims. He was familiar with all the vascular and tissue destruction and after his last tour, was recruited by the leadership team at Harbor. The current head of department was retiring and suggested his replacement. Chief of Surgery was an important post and only offered to the very best. Dr. Reinhold didn't have to be convinced and was happy not to have to transition out of the service without having a permanent position. This hospital offered him everything he was looking for, with the added prestige of being the Chief of the department.

Lamar was being transferred out of the surgery ward at UMMC to a floor below in the general ward. He would spend a couple weeks in physical therapy until he could be sent home. He had to learn how to take care of himself all over again from the vantage point of a wheelchair. He was going to spend the rest of his life in one. Fettered by the myriad tubes and drains that plagued his ability to recover at the speed he wanted, Lamar felt like he was in Hell. He was a constant strain on the hospital's resources, specifically the nursing staff, who had labeled him, "DIFFICULT PATIENT". It was in bold at the top of all the pages in his file. References to his outbursts and inability to perform many of his regular milestones, instilled a sour feeling in all the staff. When it came time for his transfer, there was a silent applause from all the people on duty that day. They figured he was the physical therapy staff's problem now. The orderlies came and helped him into a wheelchair. He was such a blatant asshole; yelling and carrying on all the way down the hall to the elevator bank. One of the nurses on the ward looked down the hall, shaking his head and saying to himself, *what a piece of shit. Probably deserved what he got!*

Compassion was lost on most of the nurses and technicians that had a part in his post surgical care.

Dr. Padashin was finishing the transitional review of Lamar's case when his cell phone rang. It was Dr. Reinhold, another surgeon that he collaborated with on occasion for hard cases, with a somewhat unexpected tone and greeting. For the first time he could recall, he was being solicited for his opinion concerning an amputation case that he was working on over at the Harbor Hospital. "Hey there Sid (short for Siddharta. He insisted his friends call him Sid because of the name butchering. It was just easier and he wasn't offended. As a matter of fact he understood because of the difficulty he first had when arriving in the US from India with english). Got a minute? I was just reviewing a case for discharge and wanted to get some feedback from you."

"Por sure Tim. Vat do I owe de pleasure ob you seeking my humble opinion? I'm usually de von asking you por your adwice."

"Well Sid, I just had this case present about a week ago with all fingers amputated from both hands. The real kicker was that all of the distal ends were cauterized with some sort of open flame. And to add to the uniqueness of this particular case, there was a fresh brand on the back. It would appear that the burns on the distal ends and the back were all performed at about the same time. Have you ever seen anything like it."

"No, I hawen't but...Dis is so pucking strange...I just treated a case ob double amputation ob da feet. De odd part being dat der vas a brand on my patient's lover back. It vas also fresh, as ip it vas completed about de same time as de feet. Tell me something Tim, do you hab de notes in front of you? Vat did the brand look like?"

"Let me see here, just give me a minute to thumb through, I made some post-its on the pages I wanted to bring to your attention. Yeah, here it is! From what I could make out in my initial report, it was sort of shaped like a shield and there was some sort of dog in the middle. I made a note of a thunderbolt and some sort of cross shaped object x'ed across the back. And also there was the number 2 and 1 on the inside of the shield on either side. Does that seem to align with what you found, Sid?" The silence was all the indication he needed. It seemed like minutes before Dr. Padashin finally spoke, only to make a simple, "HUH!" Then there was silence again that seemed like minutes. "I just don't beliewe it. Ve need to hab dis looked at furder. Do you agree Tim?"

"Uh...Yeah! I think we need to bring this to someone's attention. Got anyone in mind?"

"As it happens, I vas speaking to a couple detectives right after de surgery to seal de distal ends ob the tibia and fibula. Let me see ip I can pind deir card and I'll get back to you. Dis is highly irregular, Tim. It is blatantly obwious dat dese two cases are related in some vay. Both amputations dat were obwiously not self inflicted or indicative op an accident. Dey both had brands dat ver identical, de mark ob de perpetrator, perhaps? Anyvay, let me get a hold ob dose detectives and I'll get back to you. In de meantime, I vould keep dis to yourself. Tanks por reaching out and I vould expect a call from the detectives. By the vay, you don't mind ip I gib dem your information do you?"

" Not at all, I am just as curious as you to see where this all goes. Frankly, I'm glad that I reached out and I'm also glad you are willing to take the lead on this. I've got one hell of a caseload and this was just a giant wall in my way. I look forward to hearing what they have to say and I will be as cooperative as I am able considering my limited knowledge in the overarching case. Thanks again, Sid. I'll let you go."

He hung up the line and had to find a chair to sit down. He noticed the level of anxious excitement that was taking physical form in the small trembling of his hands. He reached into his desk drawer and pulled out a bottle of Johnny Walker Red. It was something he kept in his drawer for that particular need and only imbibed at the end of the day before he showered to head home. He also kept a baccarat cut whisky glass right next to it. It was an indulgence but one he considered warranted in his position and amount of responsibility.

After recounting the phone conversation, he opened the files and spread them out on the glass table. The two detectives, with the curiosity of children at the zoo, leaned in to see for themselves. Although there weren't any pictures, there are always sketches within the file for any abnormalities. In this case, the emergency room resident that did the initial assessment of Lamar on his admission made as detailed a sketch of the brand as she was able. The young doctor, having just graduated medical school and still very much into attention to detail, was able to capture the brand onto the paper. Both the detectives scanned over all the notes and paid particular attention to the details of the brand and its location on Lamar's body. Dr. Padashin indicated that the description he received from Dr. Reinhold over at Harbor was identical, down to the placement on the patient's back. "I don't know bout you Paul but dis some interestin shit! Oh scuse me doc, I dint mean that"

"No vorries detective, I hab heard much verse. And I agree, it is some interesting shit! (giggling by all parties)" After they all stopped laughing, the doctor started putting all the files back into the green folder and clasping them back in order. He went to his desk and took out a writing pad. With the typical handwriting that looks almost greek or latin, he scrawled the name of Dr. Timothy Reinhold along with his cell number. He handed it to Cecilia and indicated his colleague was expecting their call. "You can make arrangements to meet him. He is anxious to hear vat you have to say and is just as intrigued by de similarities between de two cases as am I. I beliewe dis is good inpormation and ip you don't mind me saying, detectives, I am certain dey are linked." Putting the pad back into the desk and closing the drawer, he got up and walked them to the door. "I vill take you back to the ER true de short cut and de rest is on you. OK? You hab my inpormation and ip you need anyting else prom me concerning dis, please don't hesitate to call my cell directly. I vant to help in dis case howewer I am needed." He showed them back into the hall, down the elevator, and out into the ER triage area.

Across town, next to a tributary of the Patapsco River, sits the small but important Harbor Hospital. It is actually just outside the city of Baltimore limits, in the county of Anne Arundel. It serves the majority of the county and shares duties with Mercy Hospital in the city to help South Baltimore as well. Some of the city ambulances that cover the areas near the line find it a closer hospital to bring in critical patients. There is no trauma center there, in fact, the only trauma unit is at the University of Maryland Medical Center.

Scott Finlay was not considered, at the time of transport, to be critical enough to be taken to the trauma center. In fact, Harbor has some of the finest surgeons in the area. One of those is Dr. Timothy Reinhold, being the Chief of Surgery and a true combat veteran. He had extensive experience in field hospitals throughout Iraq and Afghanistan. Detectives Young and Dower were in their Impala on their way to see him. He had been waiting for their call all day. After he got off the phone with his colleague Dr. Padashin over at UMMC, he was anxious to get through his daily rounds so he could devote the rest of his day preparing any files he would use during their discussion of Mr. Finlay's case. Unlike Lamar, Scott was already discharged to go home and do his physical therapy in an outpatient setting. Actually, he was sent to an assisted living and rehabilitation center in Catonsville for the rest of his treatment. He lived alone and had no immediate family in the area that could take him in so he was put on a Medicaid regulated program at this particular center.

When the detectives arrived at the administrative building across from the hospital, Dr. Reinhold was waiting for them outside the front door with a cigarette in his hand. He cordially waved them over and led them into the building. The meager building's lobby was strikingly bland compared to the opulence of the hospital's, with its marble floors and walls. His office was the typical doctor's with diplomas on the walls, pictures of extracurricular activities and family portraits, and shelves of medical journals and books. Cecilia was most impressed with the picture of the doctor, on what could only be described as the fishing trip of a lifetime, with a blue marlin hanging from a davit crane on a pier somewhere like Ocean City. She giggled to herself at the cliché. "Dr. Reinhold, thank you for lending us your valuable time. We know you are very busy so we can get right to the meat of it. Your colleague Dr. Padashin tells us that you have some information concerning one of our cases. He suggested that there were some similarities with a case that he was working on.", said Paul with a sense of urgency.

"That is correct. Please, have a seat and I'll get the file.", he answered as he ambled over to one of the several filing cabinets against the wall of framed diplomas and certificates. As the detectives were taking their seats in the chairs on the opposite side of his desk, Cecilia thought to herself how much grander Dr. Padashin's office was with the couch and coffee table. "Here it is" as he slammed the door to the cabinet. "You will find in the notes from the ER physician an indication of some sort of brand on the patient's back. This is highly irregular and I wanted to consult with my colleague Dr. Padashin to see if he had ever encountered anything of this magnitude. It was evident that the brand was as fresh as the cauterized phalangeal ends on each hand."

"Yes doctor, I would say that is highly irregular. I would also note, for the sake of context, that it is highly irregular to have your fingers removed from both hands! We have already spoken to your colleague and are convinced that there is some connection here. The brand that you indicated is fairly distinct and based on the sketches in Dr. Padashin's files it isn't a far cry to assume the brands are identical." said Cecilia. "Well I don't think we need to take up any more of your time. Thank you for your input and I am sure we will be in touch so we can get copies of your case files for our investigation."

"I will make myself available for any inquiries you may have in the future. Shall I show you out?"

"That won't be necessary doctor. Again, thank you for your time and we will be in touch." Paul and Cecilia headed for the hallway to the stairs leading to the lobby. In the stairwell, Cecilia turned to Paul and said,"Dis shit gitin weirder and weirder, u think?"

"Sure is Cel. I jus can't figur why someun ud do sometin like dis. It really give me the heebie jeebies jus thinkin bout it." They were both silent the entire way back to the office. Cecilia couldn't stop thinking about the case details and how there were so many similarities. Amputations, brands, chloroform...*it IS highly irregular*, she reinforced to herself. Meanwhile her partner, detective Young, was thinking about the steak he was going to eat when he got off. They parked the car in their assigned spot in the back of the Central Headquarters building across from the city jail, went through the central processing unit, and up to their cubicles at the Special Crimes Unit.

XVI

The following morning they were both in the office a few minutes early for their assigned shift and met at the coffee station. "Well good mornin to you Mr. Thang!" Cecilia charged in. "You know I spent a resless night las nite thinkin bout dis bullshit and ya know what? We still ain't got the report from the fingerprint lab yet on the articles from the amputation cases. Waddaya say we mosey on down there and push a bit, hey Mr. Thang?"

"Sound good Cel. I'm just a little slow gitin startin dis moanin. I had a couple after I et my steak las nite. It was da bomb! Anyway, jus gimme a couple and we can mosey on down together, K?" It was like detective Young to over imbibe on a work night so she figured he was trying to work the cases out for himself last night. It wasn't uncommon for her to encounter him with a hangover after a perplexing day. She knew him. They might as well be married during work. She knew his "tells". If they had a hard day on a particular case and he came in the next day with a hangover. She could be sure he spent the evening ruminating over the details. Most mornings, like this, she would "bust some detective balls" but this morning she had the odd feeling to leave it alone. When they finally made their way down into the basement level Paul commented, "Hey Cel, when we due for our firearms recert?" He was referring to the annual firearms training they have to pass to keep their Glock 22s.

"Probly in bout 3 months. I member we jus did it in January. Ain't it every 6 months? Or we sposed to do it every year? Time pass so quick Paul. We spose git a email anyway. I ain't gonna worry bout it. Why you askin anyway? You drinking las nite you fool? We got a job to do? Get it together Paul, I need you present!"

"Yeah, I think you right. Hey, I was thinkin las nite (Cecilia was waiting for the punchline because she knew there was something up since they were in the office upstairs), Spose there are mo dan one suspect? What we gon do?"

"Les cross dat bridge when we come to it, K, Mr. Sir? Always gittin head yoself! Les see what Mr. Cranlin got in CSI firs." she said with a stern approbation towards his still hungover attitude.

They entered the lab area and amidst the scurry of the lab technicians and interns from the local community college. After scanning the room they found Mr. Richard Cranlin, PhD. He was a short gentleman with extremely bushy hair. An unexpected trait for a person that's sole job was attention to detail. His nondescript features, except for the unkept hair, were a put off for Cecilia. She didn't care for older white men anyway but tried to keep a professional decorum when around the type. She was a detective. She felt like she earned a bit of authority over all but there were limits and when anyone was in the lab, the ultimate authority was Richard Cranlin, PhD.

They went over to the workstation. He was studiously attending to a fumaric box, looking for prints on an innocuous looking piece of metal. It was not a case that was directly related to theirs but, in his line of work, there were constant shifts in priorities and this was the one that captured his ultimate attention. "Good morning, Dr. C. I know you seem busy but do you happen to have any new information on the items we had sent down to you about the case in Druid Hill?" Cecilia was always on the fence about whether to address him as doctor or not. Her initial impression of him, with the clichéd hair and the hyperactive changes from one workstation to another, kept her in constant internal debate. She only visited the basement level lab a couple of times a month and she never recalled her mode of address on any occasion. Internally, she just rolled the dice and hoped not to offend when her mouth decided to open and discharge the salutation. Today she went with Dr. It turned out to be the right way to address him. He was busy and responded almost immediately.

"Good morning detectives. I believe I do have something that may be of use to you both. I had my best student (he liked to call the interns his students, even though he wasn't conducting any formal classes or lectures on subjects related to crime investigations), Michelle, working on latent print gathering of the garden tool that you sent over." He searched the lab, looking over all the different level cubicles impeding his direct sight.

"It was a typical garden tool that you can find in any hardware or garden store. The brand is, typically, sold in Lowes or Ace Hardware.You can probably rule out Home Depot. It seems that the inferior brands are frowned upon by that rather beastly establishment. I believe rightly so. The inferior metals and tempers I often find are always used... anyway, I digress...Michelle! Oh...Michelle! Here she comes detectives. It is such a burden to have these busy bees, humming around my lab, doing whatever they want without a consideration in the world about my space and the need to keep things professional. Really, detectives, at their age I was taking my career more seriously. They spend so much of their time carousing about, smoking cigarettes, which don't always smell like cigarettes to me, and doing some actual work in this lab. I really am coming close to my end with them...Michelle!, did you get a chance to work the garden tool I gave you yesterday? Did you find any latent prints? The detectives that are in charge of the case are here and asking if there is an update. (This was his way of prodding his 'students' and laying some of the responsibility, for the failures, to meet deadlines that riddle his department.)"

Paul was like a goldfish in a tank. He was being drawn in every direction by the myriad activities going on around him. One "student" had his white tyvex suit unzipped and drawn down around his waist, while dusting what appeared to be a dark box with some talcum-like powder. The brush he was using reminded him of some of the movies he remembered as a child growing up with the french maid, dusting the mantle, using a feather duster. The light touch used by the applicator, when administering the powder, is critical to ensure that the prints, that may or may not be present, aren't smudged beyond recognition. It is common for crime investigators to come up short most of the time when trying to obtain latent prints. The process is further complicated when the print has to be " lifted" from the object, which is often as simple as using clear tape, placed carefully on top of the dusted and now visible fingerprint (may be partial or full). Then the suspected print is "pressed" into the adhesive side and "lifted" off the object. A prepared index-type card is used to affix the final "lifted" print, sealed in an evidence container of some sort, and sent to the lab for evaluation. After being identified, the print is disseminated and input into the crime investigation computer. All of this was explained to the detectives while they were waiting for his prodigy, Michelle, to answer update questions.

The intern was remiss to divulge any definite results but alluded to the fact that there was definitely a partial print. She explained some difficulty in the lifting process and the fact that part of the print was left behind. She was running the partial print she obtained, in the system, and as of 30 minutes ago there weren't any hits. "I guess we should just give it more time. Hey Paul, les head back to the office. There are still files that we need to go through. Perhaps we can find some similarities." Cecilia was starting to lose her patience in the lab and wanted to get back to the office and use her time more efficiently. Paul, in his usual post-hangover manner, agreed to the suggestion and they both headed for the stairs.

"Alright Cel, I think we spent nuff time hir. I wouldn't mind a bit a food break anyway. My stomach talkin to me gain." They headed upstairs and spent the rest of the day pouring over the stacks of files they had, that covered both cases. Cecilia took the Finlay files and Paul the Lamar. It was approaching 5pm and Paul started squealing over the cubicle wall at Cecilia, expressing his thoughts about the possible way to link the prints to both crime scenes. There was an indication, in one of the reports from the on site CSI unit, a partial print was lifted from the metal table that Lamar was placed on and rolled around the warehouse. It was a small shot for the investigation and, since the table wasn't actually brought to the lab for processing, it was missed in the initial review of the facts.

Cecilia crept around the cubicle and was looking over his shoulder. "Great find Mr. P!" They knew it was a long shot but it was worth looking into. Paul went back down to the lab, only to find that the staff and interns had left for the evening. When he went back upstairs, he found Cecilia on the phone with the director of the lab. *Was it Dr. or Mr.?*, Paul thought as he heard her speaking into the handset of the phone. She already anticipated the vacancy for the evening and wanted to make sure they were first on the priority list for tomorrow morning. She also made a mental note to get into work 20 minutes early so she could get her coffee and be down at the lab waiting with bated breath for any results. They both retired for the evening and were adamant about being the first ones into the office in the morning.

In another part of downtown, there were two strangers meeting again. Two strangers whose lives were going to become entwined in ways that neither of them could predict. An introverted, endomorphic writer, with an overambitious ego, and another introvert that spent a large portion of his time maiming or planning to maim other human beings. What the writer didn't realize at the time was that his new friend was going to become his new liability. His life was going to change for the worse, not because he was having a meeting but because of a decision he was going to make for his sister.

Kendall was early to their meeting. It was probably because he was a writer and felt that it was the duty of the journalist to take charge of a meeting, any meeting. He probably got the idea from watching too many movies where the journalist wound up in mortal danger...*The Pelican Brief, The Parallax View, The Insider*....These were probably running through his mind while he was waiting for the stranger, he knew as Roger Stemway, that called him to show up. Garrett (Roger) explained that he had some news to share and he wanted to meet him in person. He suggested they meet somewhere where they can get something stronger than coffee this time. Garrett wanted to soften the blow of the truth and Funk's Coffee House just wasn't going to cut it.

The dark recesses of a bar in downtown Baltimore are notorious for both good and bad meetings. Some have booths and light fixtures that, both, date to the middle of the last century. Some are modern and have pool tables with surround TVs, to visualize a sports program from any angle in the room. This was a technique that bar owners figured out in the late 90's. It is better to have a large variety of sports being televised, on multiple screens, then it is to be able to listen to it. When there is something important to listen to, perhaps a final in soccer, or a division playoff in baseball, then the majority of the televisions can be diverted to that and the stereo system can be devoted to that particular game. With the other sports, viewed on the other televisions, in the background.

The one entity that profited the most from this particular revelation was the cable and satellite companies. Direct TV was notorious for marketing the Pay-per-View events, particularly big ticket fights, that came to serialize the late 90's. Entire neighborhoods were known to pitch in at the bar to ensure the costs of a particular fight were covered and the bar was able to afford broadcasting. It became commonplace for neighborhood barflies to bring covered dishes, like a potluck event, to feed the crowd during an televised fight. It was acceptable if the bar cashed in on the cost of booze and beer. It was a good trade off for the bars and kept the clientele engaged and not roaming up and down the street to every corner establishment. The bars that adopted this, early in its inception, were usually the bars that lasted the cull periods of recession.

Kendall was in a booth, in the back of one of the bars downtown, that did not adopt this new form of entertainment. The light fixture above the booth was reminiscent of a gangster movie. It only gave out enough yellowed wattage to ensure the packets you picked up were sugar and not any of that newfangled stevia or the like. The red faux leather made noise every time you shifted. It was actually vinyl but had the appearance of leather, down to the metal-faced pins that falsely attached the "pleather" to the arms of the booths. Directly across from the booth's opening was the men's room, that was in a constant state of "leaking urine". Either the smell variety or the actual liquid. Just outside the bathroom door was the cigarette machine that only took coins and had pull handles to dispense whichever flavor or brand was your poison.

He picked this place because it was dark, the beer was almost at cost, and all the customers hung in the front, at the bar. It was a remnant of the days when there were stag bars that only allowed men inside. The urine trough still surrounded the bottom edge of the bar. The brass foot rail was attached to a metal urine deflector that was tacked to the bottom of the bar on the outside, above the trough. In the old days, there was a gentlemen that actually kept those facilities clean. Of course, this was a time when peanuts were offered as a snack and the shells were scattered on the floor. It was believed that the oil from the nut shells helped to keep the floor polished. Further in the past, there may have been brass or copper spittoons that were placed at strategic areas along the trough for the tobacco chewing patrons. Spitting tobacco juice onto the floor was considered uncouth. Today, instead of a metal container on the floor, which kept it out of eyesight, they use a red plastic cup on the counter, next to their drink .

Garrett walked in, took a moment to breath, and scanned the room for the man he met earlier at the coffee house; the one that reminded him of that movie about the beatnik poets. He was particularly drawn to the metal trough that surrounded the feet of the men sitting at the bar, in stools that were older than he was alive. He noticed most of the seats were cracked and some of the stuffing was coming out. He was really impressed by the patina of the brass rails that surrounded the gentlemen's feet and the one that surrounded their elbows. His attention was again drawn to the metal-looking trough that went all the way around the L-shaped bar. He went up to the railing, near the ancient looking register, and posed a question to the man standing there with a cigarette in his mouth. "What is that metal trough for down below the bar?" he asked with all seriousness intended. His initial perception of the bar person was immediately reneged when he realized it was a woman. In a deep, unavoidable voice, that is only recognizable by the innumerable years of heavy tobacco use, the barmaid grunted, "That's where the men used to piss, sir...Are you not familiar with this?". Garrett just shook his head and decided not to chase the demon that was prodding him; to prod this old woman, or so he thought. He scanned the room again, amidst the laughter from the rest of the bar front, and found his query at the far back of the room. It was the blonde hair that ticked him off.

He wasn't very clear about the meet location but he hadn't changed much since his last meeting with him. Garrett spent some time reviewing this disparity and the lack of awareness that Kendall showed in choosing this particular meeting space. *Why is this jerk off wearing the same jacket? I know he is blonde but could he have put on a hat or done his hair differently? I can tell this kid needs some training if we are going to be working together.* Garrett (playing the role of Roger) approached the booth and couldn't help but comment on the reek of piss that was overwhelming his olfactories. He said, "Are you fucking kidding me?! You fucking cunt! (He talked like he was exchanging conversation with his battle group, in a hole in the ground, in the jungles of Columbia) You couldn't have found a bar that had a bit more life to it? This fucking thing looks like a spot out of a gangster movie!"

"Sorry, I know how important it is that we keep this incognito! I thought this would be right up your alley! Aren't you impressed? You treated me like..." He was immediately interrupted by Garret.

"You don't even know me! We can be perfectly blended and have a private conversation, in a bar, that is the complete, fucking opposite of this! We could be sitting in a sports bar, watching a game, and be entertained by beautiful ladies...Instead, you got the fucking crypt keeper here, giving me directions and helping me understand that it is, or was at one time, OK to take a fucking piss exactly where you stood! All this without having to walk back to the urine infested bathroom that you have us sitting directly beside!"

"Look man, I'm truly sorry! I had good intentions. So what have you heard about my sister's husband?" he was trying to deflect the anger that Garrett was obviously displaying.

"I spent a couple more days, after we spoke, following him. I didn't see anything out of the ordinary. I'm sorry but I don't think there is anything going on with your brother-in-law."

"That is just weird. My sister seemed convinced. I haven't spoken to her in a couple of days. Maybe I'll give her a call tomorrow and see if anything has changed. Again, I'm sorry about the place. Next time we can meet wherever you want."

"Yeah, we'll do exactly that. Get a hold of your sister and see if she has anything new to report. In the meantime, you don't need to worry yourself about places to meet. I'll give you a call in a few days to check in and see if anything has changed. In the meantime, do you have anything interesting for me?"

"Nothing that you aren't already involved with. Have you heard anything more? I would be terrified if there was any way that the police were on to me. Aren't you in the least bit worried that they are investigating these; and perhaps are onto your trail?"

"First, Kendall, keep your nose to the ground for any new leads for me. I am not done yet, ridding this community of the dregs that are taking up valuable space in my mind. Second, I don't put a lot of metaphysical weight on the police finding anything that would lead them to me. I was careful about how I planned and executed my work. So, as you can see, by my demeanor, I am not in the least worried about it. Thirdly, Kendall, I will keep tabs on your brother-in-law for a little while longer but don't hold your breath. I am pretty sure this guy is clean. If he isn't, then we'll just have to see. Now, I'm gonna leave first because I don't want to spend another minute in this cholera trap. You follow after me in about 5 minutes. I want you to sit here and think about the idiotic decision you made in having us meet here and then I want you to wipe it from your mind... not only for now but in the future. Places like this are for the lower forms of barfly that would rather waste away in a darkened tomb, then come out and enjoy the beautiful world that is all around them. We'll talk..." With that he slipped out of the smoke infused bar to the hacking coughs and eternal laughing coming from the seats near the door.

XVII

The Hampton Inn is pretty consistent for the Baltimore Convention Center area hotels. The choices are limited to the usual; double beds, a queen room, or a king. The hotels don't push for luxury but rather utility. Most are serving the ballfields, the convention center, or the civic center's many events. Camden Yards is close.The railroad museum is within this area. Its iconic, round building helps it stick out from the rest of the tourist attractions. Most people are intrigued by the locomotive museum. The rail yard, nearby, will accept over 2000 different cars, for sorting and storing. After sorting, they are assigned an engine and transported to the final destination. Baltimore is one of the few stations on the East that, in close proximity to the water, is capable of handling a very high volume of cargo. The train museum has been an east Baltimore staple for longer than the stadium. The hotel that Garrett is watching from across the street, is a product of the city expansion.

Steam was coming off the mirror's surface. Tom hesitated, then brushed his forearm against the mirror in an arc. Temporarily opening the grey vapor, attached so delicately onto the silvered glass, Tom looked passed the image. He looked into the half opened curtain that obscured his view from behind. Trish was in the bathroom taking a shower. Steam was pouring out of the doorway that she left ajar. Tom was trying to fix his hair and kept having to wipe the mirror. He was anxious about his trip today and couldn't wait to get the rest of his clothes on and leave. Trish loved to keep him on the hook and danced around the room naked when she got out of the shower. She always had some semblance of 80's music playing on the radio so she could show off her moves. The room was on the 7th floor and faced the old train station. It was converted into the ball field recognized today, as Camden Yards. Third base wasn't far from the corner of the wall, as all ballfields are meant to be.

Garrett could only wish to have a seat there and the chance to catch a foul ball. He spent most of the evening in the parking lot facing the hotel so he could see the one, solitary window that gave him a view into the room he was watching all night. He missed the baseball game because he was trying to figure out where the best place was for him to settle down and surveil for the evening. It turned out the young lady at the desk wasn't overly curious and open to giving out the information relating to Tom and his room. It wasn't a great Hotel. It was, however, both a convenience and a coincidence that Tom picked a room that overlooked the outfield and was in good alignment from the main parking lot to the Yard. The tall brick structures that make up the old Camden Train Station are an iconic part of the park that people know today. It is also not a stretch to be at the hotel across the street on the 7th floor and be able to watch most of the game, especially at night when they turn the lights on. It isn't uncommon to see a foul ball come within inches of falling into the street from that side of the hotel. Some of the local boys even loiter in front, to fight for the balls that do make it outside of the Yard walls.

Tom wiped the surface of the mirror and took a closer look at the hardened monster that was staring back at him. He knew he wasn't really a monster but was feeling like that towards his wife and family, now that he was involved with Trish. His view from the window was so unreal that he took it for granted when there was some generalized shouting from the stands. The Orioles were having a regular season game with the Tampa Bay Rays and the stadium noises weren't anything that couldn't be heard for miles around that part of the city.

What he didn't know was that there was a small light coming from the parking lot on the third base line. Tom was honed in on this vehicle and, without his normal level of caution, he had the window shades wide open and the lights on full blast. With Trish in the bathroom and the steam rolling out, the outside window was starting to form a bit of a haze. The noises from the stadium were still at full volume. Most people that are trying to be secretive know that lights which are left on in a room, leave drastic shadows in the surrounding areas.

Garrett spent his entire military career learning the difference between shadows and light. He used this advantage to decimate more than one drug lab. Most of his operations were done at night but the ones that had to be performed during the daylight hours were always performed with the shadow as an ally. Garret only had so many friends in the civilian world and only a few of them were actually aware of his propensity for living in the shadows. He spent many nights out, consumed with how he was going to be able to sneak around in the shadows, only to find that the party was lit like a stadium. His only job was to drink himself into oblivion and not a single person was paying attention to whether he was even there or not.

Outside in his car, Garrett was putting the field glasses down on the dashboard. He realized that his next job was in front of him. He started to get sick and held his stomach while he leaned out of the window. What kind of punishment did this person deserve? His last 2 shitheads were men. This was a woman! *How in the world should I deal with this. I never did anything like this to a woman before.* The struggle between the real man and the chivalrous man were tugging at his inner feelings. It is hard enough to be in a verbal fight with a woman but to get into a physical altercation brought up feelings of his mother. Every guy he ever talked to, while deployed, was in one stage or another of emotional turmoil concerning their mothers. Garrett kept flashing to Ray Romano and his relationship with his showtime mom.

His mother was a cancer victim when he was young. She suffered horribly and died very quickly after she had a nodule removed from her breast. Apparently it was too late and the disease had spread throughout her body before she even had a chance to face it. He didn't even think about his mother's breasts or that they could actually kill her. He was busy with boy things and never realized that a woman could die from tit cancer. It was a point in his life that left him numb. For a young man of 16, losing your mother is life altering. One might say that he was stuck in this time for his adult life.

When he went off to the military, he never really got over the loss of his mother. It was one of the things that drove him to continue through his special operations training. His father, basically, checked out of the picture when she passed. Going through special forces selection, with this kind of trauma in the back of your mind, can actually be a reason to continue fighting through the anguish and pain. The cadre that run these schools usually get a dossier full of everything you've ever done in your entire life. So when Garrett got to the SEER portion of his operational training, he spent most of it in a box, crying about how these people knew the things they did and why they were breaking him down into the smallest piece of shit he could possibly be. When he went to the interrogation portion of the training, he broke down. The cadre didn't let up either. They watched him flood with tears and then cranked him with more gut rearranging questions. This went on for what felt like days. Periods of light and periods of darkness. The in between parts were always full of yelling and shouting in languages that he was unfamiliar with. He caught riffs of Russian and Arabic but for the most part, were languages he had not heard before. Perhaps they were bullshit languages. He only went to Spanish language school for his Special Forces Training. It was a "romantic" language and based mostly on latin. He could meekly translate his shitty Spanish into Italian, Portuguese, and any Latino derivative, if he tried. There were always words and phrases in the local dialects that he didn't fully understand but for the most part he could piece together a sentence from those languages. This was different. They weren't speaking in a tongue he couldn't cobble.

He cried most of the time he spent in the dog houses he was placed in. Not the kind of full bodied crying and uncontrollable tears but a continual stream of watery eyes that he had to keep wiping. When the cadre came by, he assumed every couple of hours because time seems to stand still in those situations, the classical music wasn't blaring in the background. They would beat the dog house and shout obscenities that he never paid attention to. On his final day of SEER, he was taken to a room, stripped completely naked, chained to the ceiling with bindings that barely allowed him to keep his toes on the ground, and put under extreme physical and mental pressure. They shouted demands at him in just about every language he couldn't understand. The last cadre came in and started shouting in english about how his family was going to die and he was gonna cut his balls off and feed them to him. Of all the time he spent in SEER, this was the most terrifying to him.

It is pretty common for the last day to be the worst. This was known as "naked day" and you are stripped not only of your dignity but of your ability to control your core temperature. Garrett was so cold, his penis had shriveled up and his balls were basically just a thick layer of skin between his legs. The cadre brought over a machete and started to scrape it back and forth around his groin area. The entire school was supposed to see how long you could survive without revealing detailed information. Garret didn't let on a thing other than his serial number and rank. After a week of pure torture and a final naked destitution, he gave up his name. It was expected that everyone would break at some point. For some it was as early as day one and others made it until the end. Garrett went all the way to the bitter end; stripped naked, hanging by his arms, finally broke into tears and gave his real name, an inevitable reality of the program. He was sobbing uncontrollably and just kept saying his name over and over again...

Garrett was determined to make this right. He had to continue his "work" and rid his local community of the evils that he believed were ruining it. He waited for them to leave the hotel so he could find out where Trish lived and was particularly careful not to follow too close. He never received any formal training in operational or technical driving, just the same training from his high school driving program that most of the people in the United States have. Garrett passed his driving test the first time so he was proud of that. He didn't get any personalized instruction from his father because his father was never around, instead, relied on the driving school to learn the basics. He was a considerate driver and always applied the principles of defensive driving to his daily excursions.

Garrett noticed they were turning onto 695, the beltway that goes around Baltimore City. They were heading towards Dundalk on the east side. They got off on Merritt Boulevard and were heading to the Gray Manor development. This was basically a middle class, white, immigrant neighborhood, made up of people that were retired; of German and Polish decent. The cookie cutter single family homes were all built some time in the early 60's. He pulled over at the next intersection to a view straight through the ball field at the middle school there. He watched them pull into a house on the other side of the field. Trish got out of the passenger side of the Nissan and walked around to the driver's side. She stooped over into the window and gave Tom a kiss. As he backed out of the driveway Trish turned around and gave a final wave. Garrett decided he would find a better place to sit on the house for a while and see if there were any other people living there. He watched Tom's Nissan pull away and started to daydream about ways to make this woman suffer. Should he pluck out that diseased tongue she used to kiss that married man? What about removing both of her eyes so she couldn't see for the rest of her life? He floated off into a cat nap and spent the rest of the light hours snoring at the clouds in the sky.

Garrett woke to the sound of cicadas chirping in the trees that lined the street he was on. The air was thick and humid; it smelled like rain. He looked across the avenue towards the house Trish entered and noticed a light was still on in the front room. The clock on his dash radio said 9:22. He looked over at his watch and confirmed that it was completely wrong. It was only 7:46. He looked for a pen in the glove box so he could properly set the clock. As he pulled the box open, papers that pertained to the car and his registration came spilling out to reveal the pistol that he kept in there. His Glock was always loaded and he knew he was taking a chance carrying it like that, especially in Maryland. The gun laws are strict and skewed strongly towards the government. Obtaining a carry permit is basically impossible unless you can prove that you carry a lot of cash, back and forth to the bank, for business purposes. Garrett didn't have that option and knew if he was pulled over the jig would be up. Instead of wasting a lot of brain power worrying about it, he grabbed one of the several free pens he got from this or that booth at the Fells Point Festival and shoved the papers back in. After he set the clock he took one more look back up at the house and noticed that the light was out. The house was completely dark and he assumed that Trish had gone to bed for the evening. He decided he would head home himself and come back in the morning

He woke up with a purpose and decided to make some breakfast. He would give Kendall a call and tell him the news. He had been following his brother-in-law around for weeks with no results and yesterday he hit the jackpot. "Good morning Kendall, I have some interesting news for you," he said as he sipped his second cup of java. "I followed your brother-in-law yesterday and he met with that woman, Trish, at the Hampton Inn near Camden Yards. I stayed there all night after the game and had perfect eyes on their room from the parking lot." He was starting to get excited at the idea of spilling this news to Kendall and hearing his reaction. "They were in the room all night and left at checkout the next day. I followed them to a house in Dundalk. She got out and he drove off. I left later that evening when she went to bed." Kendall was silent the entire time he was relaying his report. After what felt like several minutes Kendall replied, "Well this is not what I expected. I don't know how I am going to tell my sister. She has been settling down a bit after I told her that there wasn't anything to worry about. She was convinced something was going on with Tom but I just couldn't believe it. This is going to devastate her. I feel like calling her up right now so she can confront that son of a bitch!"

"Just take a breath Kendall. I know this must come as a shock but we can take care of this. Why don't you wait till tomorrow to tell her about the infidelity? In the meantime I'll come up with a plan to ensure that Trish is out of the picture. Are you sure you don't want me to punish Tom as well? I mean this IS a two way street...this type of thing?" Garrett was serious about the question. He hadn't formed a solid interpretation of his moral compass yet but was sure this situation was a two way road. His last two victims elicited a much different feeling than this. He was absolute in his position and there were no residual feelings. This felt more intimate. He was involved, emotionally, with a person that he just met. His capacity for destruction without complicity was irresolute. He was formed in a compartmentalized world and would continue to live in the same. Tom's potential suffering was nothing more than a compartment, for Garrett.

"Absolutely not! It is already going to be a strain on my sister when she finds out about this. I don't want her to have to worry about him and the kids. She can't be a single mother, Roger. I appreciate the offer but I don't want anything to happen to Tom. My sister will deal with him in her own way. God only knows what that will be but I am sure he won't ever forget it. Yeah, my sister will take care of him and do what she thinks is right. I just want to make that woman suffer for causing this pain to my sister. You can understand that, right, Mr. Stemway?"

"Sure man. I understand." His mind crept off, again, to the jungle. He sat down and started to smell the undergrowth. The dense, overpopulated undergrowth. All the things that could kill you in the jungle, originated in the undergrowth. Garrett went to the undergrowth of Columbia. At night, it was so dark that he could barely make out his hand, 5 inches from his face. The monkeys howled, the frogs moaned, and the spiders tittered. *Oh God! please don't let the spiders touch me tonight! I'll do anything you ask but please let me sleep for a couple hours.*

Garrett finally woke up from his dream state to Kendall's voice. He was checking the inside of his pants for any spiders that decided to take a spin around his groin. His flashbacks were becoming so real that he couldn't help but check himself for critters. Time on the floor, sleeping, is just time for the creatures to infiltrate. "Let me finish my breakfast and I'll figure out where to go with this. In the meantime, figure out how your going to break it to your sister and then prepare for the coming storm. This is good business. I was built to take care of situations like this and I fully intend on taking this bitch out of the equation. You can assure your sister that the woman will disappear. Well, maybe don't tell her anything about that. Let's just keep that to ourselves. Anyway, my eggs are getting cold and I've got a lot of planning to do." He felt a phantom touch on his left ankle and reached down to sweep it away. Spiders are an acceptable crawler. It is the snake tongues that raise hairs on the back of his neck. *Please God, let it be a spider...I just can't handle a snake right now...* "Good luck Kendall, with your sister I mean. I'll keep you informed as things progress. Until then... just take some time to think about how to tell her." With that Garrett hung up the phone and finished his breakfast. Between the ankle itching and the groin checking, he needed some time to come up with the perfect way to destroy this bitch and he intended on making that happen as soon as he could.

Garrett spent the next evening scoping out the house in Dundalk that Trish had entered. He sat across the street, adjacent to the baseball diamond that served the high school. He was wide awake, having taken some amphetamine pills that were readily available at the local Rexall drugstore. He smirked at the bottom of the tagline that said: "The Family Druggist". It was ironic that he was able to purchase OTC amphetamines, Dexatrim. They use to call it speed. It was packaged and marketed for weight loss but it was the go to drug for all the college kids during exam week. It would keep the average person awake for over 24 hours and enable them to study for the week without any need to rest. There are the days when an "endless pot of coffee" are indicated but there are also days when there is a need to stay awake and cram. Some were able to afford paying the premium for Dexatrim to keep awake for the next week or so. One box of the drug was around $8 and there were 10 pills that could be spread over a couple of days. It was a miracle most of the people that used this product didn't develop heart related issues later in their lives.

He was sure, after several nights of surveillance that Trish, the home wrecker, was alone. He never saw anyone coming or going from there except her. He was now shifting his thoughts to a plan for the kidnapping. *Should I just break in and work on her in her own house? I don't see any immediate cameras but the neighbors have "Ring" doorbells across the street. The angles aren't perfect but they would pick me up if I use the front door. I'll sneak around the back later tonight and see if there is a way to gain entrance from there. No cameras in the back, I hope.* As the sky turned from a dark blue to black, the street lamps came on one by one.

He walked around the block and found an alley between the front and back streets. All the homes in this neighborhood were back to back. An alley, used by the municipal trash collectors, separated them. The streetlamp that lit the alley was a few houses away and there was a conspicuous shadow that cast directly over the gate leading to Trish's yard. The old chainlink fence was in bad shape and loosened from some of its anchor points. He didn't want to make a bunch of noise trying to scale it so he tried the gate. To his surprise it was in relatively good working order and he gently opened it.

He entered the grassy back yard. It hadn't been cut in a while so he kept to the edges to keep from making indentations in the tall grass. He didn't see any signs of a dog and during his surveillance he didn't hear or see her walking one. The back door had an overhead light that was off with several concrete steps leading to the stoop. Walking around to the far side of the house he came to the dining room window with the shades wide open. He was able to peer inside and see that Trish was laying on the couch, in the living room, watching TV. There was an episode of Seinfeld and she was giggling at the way Kramer was shaking around Jerry's kitchen, dancing to some imaginary music in his head as he looked for something to eat in the fridge.

Garrett made his way back to the rear door and opened the screen. He jostled the handle and as he expected, it was locked. Because of the age on the door and its lack of proper maintenance over the years, there was a significant gap between it and the old wooden jamb. He took out a library card and tried to slide it between the gap that was created. It went right in and he shimmied the card down where the latch inserts into the strike plate on the doorjamb. With a bit of force he was able to retract the latch enough to disengage it from the jamb but the deadbolt was on and he couldn't open it.

In his jacket pocket he brought with him his basic lock pick set. He unsnapped the leather case and unfolded the book-like wrap. The picks were all organized according to their purpose, with the tension wrench on the immediate left. Shaped, single-edged picks on the left and rakes on the right. The double-paged "bible" was rife with possibilities. He searched the right side and slid out his Bogota Rake. He loved it, if for any other reason than he spent the last couple of years in the country for which it was named. The Columbian snake. The rake pick to beat all picks. It is an exaggerated snake rake that he has had a lot of success with in the past. He found it especially useful for the pin sets on the Kwikset brand locks, which he noticed this particular deadbolt lock to be. It is a common brand sold in most home improvement centers like Home Depot and Lowes.

With the tension rod in place, it only took a couple in and out strokes with the pick to be able to turn the deadbolt. It was tight because of misalignment in the door. He gave the handle a slight pull as he turned the lock and it easily and quietly disengaged from the strike. One more time with the card and he had the door ajar. He could hear the tv in the background.

He silently opened the door; just enough to be able to poke his head in. He felt the breeze of a fan blowing in the kitchen and assumed there must be one on the ceiling. He scanned the kitchen and it appeared to be well used and there were some dishes in the sink. She must have just finished dinner and laid down to relax before going up to bed. He could just make out a light coming through the entranceway leading to the dining room. The TV was still on and he heard a commercial for some type of medication. He slowly closed the door and held the screen door back so it wouldn't slam shut. He knew that access to the house wouldn't be too difficult and decided that he would confront her in the house. He wasn't sure if he wanted to do what he was going to do here or take her somewhere else like he did with Scott. He was getting tired and knew that the excitement he was feeling would soon wear off. He was going to crash.

A brief scan of the jungle floor was the scene in his mind now. So much undergrowth. He reached over to the bush at his right and felt the pierce of a thorn. When he looked, the entire branch had large thorns growing from its base. He started to sweat as he looked around. All the branches he saw were lined with dagger-like thorns. He couldn't place his hands anywhere without piercing them. His heart started to race and the sweat was dripping from his forehead. his palms were swimming in sweat. *God! Just help me get out of here. I just need to make it home!*

His eyes started to focus again, he realized he was standing in the ball field at the school, across the street from Trish's house. He decided to head home, get some sleep, and come up with the rest of the plan. It was near midnight when he finally got to sleep and used the thought of torturing this girl as fuel for his dreams. The nightmare of the jungle was no more that night. It would follow him for the rest of his life. The fear was real and haunted most of his dreams but they were filled with plans now. No empty spaces for the creatures to fill. He had plans and would use them to keep the jungle out.

In the morning, Garret had an epiphany about how he was going to make this person pay. He watched a tv program, a few weeks ago, about a boy that had a face transplant. This had been in the back of his mind since. What if he were to perform a full facial excision? *This bitch is ruining lives because she looks attractive and has some charm. If I take that away from her then she won't be able to charm anyone anymore. I need to do some research because I know that the head is gonna bleed a lot. This might be my best plan yet,* he thought to himself. As he was grabbing his computer off the coffee table, it dawned on him that he could use some lidocaine with epinephrine. Injected under the skin, to close off the capillaries and smaller vessels, it will keep her from bleeding too much. He went to his bathroom cabinet to see if he had any and right there on the shelf next to his suture kit was a small vial of exactly that. *The plan is coming together and I want to start as soon as everything is in place.* He started gathering the rest of the supplies he would need to complete this new project. The brand was already in the trunk of his car along with the MAPP gas torch to heat it up with. The Glock was still in the glove box. He went out to the trunk to verify if the bag with the chloroform was still there. He added a small bottle of saline solution and rolls of gauze to wrap her face with after the removal. All he needed now was to set a time and commit to the mission. He decided that he would pull the trigger in two nights. If he waited until she went upstairs to bed he might have a better chance of getting her while she was asleep. The element of surprise was going to be a key factor in the success of this mission. He put everything into the bag in his trunk and wanted to give Kendall a call and let him know the good news.

His first attempt at hailing Kendall ended in a busy signal. On the second attempt a few minutes later he reached his voicemail. *Why didn't he pick up? I don't want to leave a message on his phone.* "Hey Dickhead! It's your partner. Call me back. I've got some new developments to go over with you." Garrett kept it short and decided it was best to keep details over the phone to a minimum. The plan was set and the gears were already in motion.

XVIII

Tuesday, 2100p, 3 blocks from Trisha's home

Garrett parked his car far enough away to keep the immediate neighbors on Trisha's street from getting suspicious. He took a couple swigs from the same bottle of Red that he kept in the day bag. He noticed this time that he wasn't as anxious as his previous encounters. He held his hand up in front of the steering wheel and it was perfectly still. Reaching across the dash, he opened the glove box and removed the Glock. He pushed the magazine release button with his right thumb and dropped the magazine. Garrett checked the tiny holes on the side of the clip that indicated the ammunition left inside. He only had 10 rounds in the clip. Pushing the slide back with his hand, he thumbed the slide lock and revealed an empty breech. He inserted the clip and released the slide with a loud click and authoritative snap to his wrist, chambering a round. He reached in the backseat and grabbed the bag. Inside, he inventoried his supplies: Chloroform and rag, brand and torch, bottle of lidocaine with epinephrine and a 20cc hypodermic needle, 4 packs of gauze roll bandages, and a scalpel with number 10 blade. He opted for this blade instead of the number 11 to keep from poking holes in the skin as he dissected the dermis from the fascia. Not having done this before, he assumed there might be some difficulties in the separation. He stepped out of the car, tucked the Glock into his back waistband, and donned the bag.

The backyard was exactly as he remembered it from a couple of days ago. He made his way through the rusty gate and up to the back door. Waiting for a couple of minutes, listening with precision and intent, he decided it was safe to start opening the door. He removed the rake and tension wrench from his jacket and worked on the deadbolt. As before, it only took a couple in and out movements to line up all the pins. The tension wrench twirled around and the lock was disengaged. He placed the rake back into his jacket and got out his wallet. The library card had seen better days but was still stiff enough to give him the leverage he needed to push the latch back from the doorjamb. The door surged open about an inch and started to make a creeping sound. Grabbing the doorknob with bated breath, he held the door still for a couple of minutes while he tried to slow down his breathing. *That was close. Thank God the neighbors keep to themselves around here or this might have been a disaster from the start.*

He slowly opened the door and peered into the dark kitchen. There was nothing but silence and darkness. The living room was also empty with a small beam of light entering through a crack in the drapes on the picture window behind the couch. The only sound he could make out was the ticking of the mechanical clock that was hanging on the wall above the mounted phone in the kitchen. The mechanical whir of the clock gears seemed to keep him calm and ensured him that he was alone on the floor. He headed to the living room and found the bottom of the stairs. Placing his hand on the newel post he paused, took in a deep breath, and listened for any "out of the ordinary" sounds coming from the top of the stairs. This was his moment and he took the time to soak it all in. He felt a kind of pride in himself for taking on this particular project. It was certainly the first time he would be doing something this extreme and he only hoped it would go as smoothly as the two previous times. They say it takes 3 times to become a serial killer. Since he wasn't killing anyone, he wondered if the same applied to him in the form of a serial disabler. This time he was taking away a valuable prize, not necessarily permanently disabling someone but certainly changing their life forever. It was something that Trisha valued and used to manipulate men into doing what she wanted; her looks. He knew it would be as catastrophic to lose her face as it did for Scott to lose his fingers.

The silence was exactly what Garrett needed. It was like a warm blanket wrapped around him on a cold night. He felt safe in the silence and started up the stairs, one at a time. He walked as close to the outside edge of the tread as possible to avoid any creaking. The area right next to the wall is the best because that is where the treads are secured to the wall, keeping them fairly stable and less able to move and shift under the weight of a footfall. Garrett managed to make it all the way to the top of the stairs without a peep. All of the doors were opened, to his delight, so he wouldn't have to worry about them making any sounds from bad hinges.

He worked his way from door to door until he found her bedroom. Although she wasn't snoring, he could tell she was in a deep sleep by the way she was breathing so lightly. He thought how silly it was that the lighter the breath, the deeper the sleep. He watched lots of his comrades sleep in the jungle. If they weren't snoring, which he normally stopped by placing his hand over their mouth until they woke up. Wide-eyed and tense, he had his finger over his mouth for the international symbol of "Shut the Fuck Up!" and they immediately realized where they were.

It was dangerous in the jungle. Even to sleep, it was a dangerous prospect. Everything was trying to kill you. *Spiders. Oh God!! Please don't let the spiders crawl in my open mouth while I'm asleep!* He was falling back into his anxieties again. The jungle would stay with him for the rest of his life. She was on her right side facing the back wall of the room. *Her back is to me so this couldn't have gone any better. This is the moment of truth.* He thought as he removed the bag and took out the chloroform and rag. He opened the bottle and splashed a copious amount onto the rag. The fumes rose immediately into his nose and almost made him cough out loud. He turned his head towards the top of the stairs and released his breath as slowly as possible. This alleviated the need to cough as he replaced the bottle of chloroform back into the bag. He set the bag down just outside the bedroom door and started to make his way across the room.

Two steps and the floor gave way underneath his feet. A loose floorboard made a loud creak and he immediately lifted his foot off the spot. His anal sphincter tightened and he got a cramp in his thigh that felt like he was stabbed with a kitchen knife. It took all his energy to put his leg back down as he massaged his thigh. He looked up at Trisha and she hadn't missed a beat of her breath. A small snort and movement of her arm caused Garrett to have another spasm in his leg. He grabbed it and started squeezing the spot that tightened up. This was the kind of stress he was trained for and fortunately he learned to ignore most pain while operating. He was still a few feet away from the bed and had to make a quick scuffle to reach the edge.

He reached over her head and placed the rag over her mouth and nose. She momentarily and instinctively reached for his arm but within seconds was limp and unconscious from the rather strong fumes that entered her airway. The action was somewhat immediate and her being asleep certainly helped in keeping the fight short. He left the rag there for a couple more seconds to give her an extra dose of the anesthetic. Moving her onto her back, he removed the blanket she was under and brought her to the edge of the bed.

He was trying to figure out how to make himself comfortable and noticed a stool over at her vanity that would fit the bill perfectly. He pulled it next to the bed and checked the height. He guessed the whole process would take about an hour and he didn't want to be around any longer than he had to. He retrieved the bag from the hallway and took out the lidocaine and needle. He just filled the entire syringe and started working his way around the perimeter of her face. The tiny needle holes bled a combination of red and clear. They leaked for a few seconds as the temporary bubbles, formed from the liquid being injected under the skin, seeped out. He kept at this until he had a small outline all the way around her face. *Botox but NOT!*, he thought and then giggled to himself. He filled the syringe one more time and started to arbitrarily apply the local anesthetic to areas within the perimeter he formed. There are so many small vessels feeding the facial muscles that this was going to be a trial and error game for him.

He found the scalpel and made the first incision just under her left ear down to her chin following the jawbone. To his great delight there was very little bleeding. He decided to play it safe and opened a pack of gauze pads he brought with him for that exact reason. A small dab and it didn't even look like there was a cut there. He continued around the perimeter he formed with the needle until he met the original start of the cut. The fun part was going to begin now...

Garrett looked over at the digital clock on the nightstand. It was 2230. He had been at it for over an hour. He was working on the last section around her right eye. The rest of the skin was already peeled away and sitting, upside down, over her left cheek. All the medical books and anatomy texts in the world couldn't prepare him for this view. Everything was various shades of red, with the white fascia distinct from the rest. There were a few fat deposits around her eyes but other than that, it was a deeply perfused red. He had to use the lidocaine a couple more times to stave off the blood that was leaking from areas around the cheeks. He was learning a lot about the vascular anatomy of the face. He hadn't really processed what he was looking at and all he could think of was hamburger meat. Chopped steak. Blood red pulp. He dabbed a few more times around the last eye and removed the skin completely. *What the fuck am I going to do with this? Feed it to one of the neighborhood dogs? No way, too risky. I'll just put it in a plastic grocery bag and tape it up. Any random trashcan should work for the disposal.* He thought as he did some final cleaning of the exposed fascia. Stepping back he realized the enormity of the effects this was going to have on her. She will certainly require some plastic surgery and skin grafts. He flashed back to some of the IED pictures he saw, post-incident. Severe burn victims that had their faces reconstructed. He was paying particular attention to her nose. It is unsettling to see a person that is missing their nose. After he removed the skin and cartilage, he was staring into two distinct holes in her face that led to her cranial sinuses and brain. It was really a site to behold.

He got the gauze out of the bag and unwrapped the rolls. He soaked the gauze in some of the saline solution he brought with him. It would help keep the bandages from sticking to the open wound. He started to wrap her head like a mummy. It took all 4 rolls to fully cover the area and he left one eye opening for her to see when she woke up. The pain she was going to be in was going to be excruciating when all the anesthetic wears off. Anyone that has skinned themselves on the concrete can relate. "Road Rash" is what they used to call it when Garrett was a kid. Riding bikes down the hill and skidding would occasional lead to a good 2-3 foot slide down the asphalt. In shorts this was not cool. He cringed as he thought about it and finished the wrapping. *Time to mark my work,* he thought.

He reached into the bag and took a couple of calming slugs on the Johnnie Walker. He put the stool back by the vanity and turned Trisha onto her stomach. Some of the blood had already seeped through the gauze and was smearing onto her pillow. He took out the saturated rag and gave her a couple more seconds of the anesthetic. She let out a small moan and was immediately out again. He fired up the torch and started heating the metal. It didn't take very long before the brand was glowing a white orange and the heat coming off was making Garret sweat. He walked over and lifted her pajama top. He placed the brand between her shoulder blades as the smoke began to rise. Once again, that smell induced some dry heaving in Garrett and he did his best to fight the urge to throw up all over her. It only took about 5 seconds and the skin around the brand was starting to darken. The indentation it left in her back was the deepest yet. The figure on her blistered skin was as clear as if it had been drawn on. Her beautifully fair color was now screaming red and crusted black. Garrett didn't take another moment to ponder the work. Packing up the bag, he carried the brand, still extremely hot, down the stairs and to the kitchen sink to cool it off under the flow of the faucet.

XIX

Cecilia made it to work early this day. She had planned on being in so that she could get to the lab early and get in front of the queue for important crime scene business. She was interested in the results for the fingerprint matching that the lab was working on. When she arrived, one of the interns was busily working on a project involving ballistics for another case. She walked over to the table and with all the positivity she could muster this early in the morning she asked, "Excuse me Miss, I am detective Dower. I was curious if the results for the Jenkins case have been processed. It was a set of fingerprints that were lifted from a table down at the shipyard. Are you familiar with this?"

" Yes detective, just give me a minute to find the folder. It has been a busy week for all of us down here in the lab and we are trying to keep our heads above water." she explained with a hesitation that only a young hard working female can intimate. "Here it is...It appears that there was a match found with this and another case. It says here there was a Finlay case that involved some amputated fingers. Well they found some prints that had a 97.28% match. They were both partials and were in good enough condition for the computer to be able to get points off of."

"Well that is exactly what I was hoping for. Was there a match found in the database so we can get a name?"

"That information I don't have here in this file. Perhaps you can wait until Mr. Cranlin gets in and ask him." The young intern was getting uncomfortable answering Cecilia's questions and started to recede back to her original work.

"May I have the case file?"

"If it's all the same to you I would like to pass this to Mr. Cranlin and he can send the completed work up to you."

"That will be fine. Thank you for your time and I'll be waiting for the file to arrive later today if possible." Cecilia started up the stairs to let Paul know what they had found. She was anxious to get a name out of all this so that the crest of the work can be reached and the downward climb to closing this case could begin. She realized this was the kind of case that got people promoted to the upper echelons of the department. A small smile crossed her face as she thought about the idea of making Captain in the near future. She always saw herself in an Executive position and spent most of her career trying to get there. This case was her ticket to the top. She wasn't about to flub it up now.

Paul was waiting for her to come back up from the bowels of the building and greeted her with a smile when he saw that she made it in as she said she would. " Hey there Miss Missy! I ain't think you had it in ya to make it dis early in the mornin."

"Oh, shut it! I can make it hir as early as I need to. You know I wanna be firs in de lab so dat we get a jump on da fingerprintin."

"And, How it go?"

"Well it pears dere was a high probility for de match tween de two prints dat were found in de two cases. Wir just waitin to find out if der is a match to someone already in da database. We gonna get the results an case file later today, accordin to da intern dat was workin down der. She wanna wait fir Cranlin to rive fo sharin da file."

"Sound good, Cel. What we do in da meantime? Is der anything else we gon get from da victims? Would it be a good idea ta head back out an see if dey can member anythin else? Or we just be chasin our tails?"

"No Paul, I think we should spend some time pourin over da files an see if der any more similarities in da cases sides da fingerprints. We might be missin some fin jumpin out at us. Both da victims pear to have a brand in de same place on de back. The brand pears to be da same. Dey both knocked out with chlorform on deir lab results and dey symptoms wakin up and rivin at da hospital. I just wonder if der anythin else...Les get da files and go to da conference room. We can spread em out an look for sumfin. Dey say, 'Two sets eyes is better dan one.'" Paul grabbed the files off his desk and headed for the conference room down the hall.

It appeared like hours before the phone rang at the conference room table. The call was forwarded from Cecilia's desk. It was Richard Cranlin down in the lab. "Detective Dower, I believe we have a match. There is a 98.65% match found in one of the databases used by the DOD. The gentleman's name is Garrett Kunter. He is a veteran of the Army. His file says he was a medical sergeant with the 7th Special Forces Group out of Florida. He currently lives here in Baltimore. If you come downstairs I can go over it with you and give you the rest of the lab file."

"Paul and I will be right down Dr. Cranlin. Thank you for the call." They both put all the files back together and cleaned the rest of the table off. Cecilia gave him a wink and they both made their way down the stairs to get the answers they had worked so diligently for.

The detectives were excited for the lead. Once they left the lab offices, they headed straight for the Impala. Cecilia wanted to get a jump on questioning the suspect, Garrett. They headed south out of the city towards Glen Burnie. Turning off on 12th Street in Brooklyn Park they headed over to the address they were given as his house. It was a nice cape cod style on the corner. There was a detached garage, in the rear, that appeared empty. No dogs in the yard either. They went to the front door and knocked. No answer. Paul gave a stiffer knock and called out "Baltimore City Police". Still no answer. Perhaps he was out. "Hey Paul, les head back to da car and sit for a bit and see if he pull up." They both headed back to the car and just before she pulled the handle on the door, her phone rang. It was their Captain calling to tell her another possible victim turned up at Mercy Hospital downtown. He wanted them to get there and follow up, to see if there was any relation to the cases they were working on. All they knew was the victim had her face removed and was in serious condition. She was being prepped for surgery to take grafts and place them on the open areas of her face. They got back in the car and headed to the city. Neither of them said a word the entire trip.

Paul was driving, as usual, and parked the car in the lot down the street from the hospital. They headed to the main entrance to get the information from the receptionist. "Good morning, how may I direct you?" the gentleman at the reception desk asked.

"We are here concerning a patient that was just admitted for a missing face." Paul said as delicately as he could find the words for. The receptionist saw the badges, which they both removed from their shirts, and realized they were there to investigate. It was already all over the hospital that someone arrived without a face. It had even trickled down to the janitorial staff as the two currently in the lobby couldn't help but stare at the officers as they questioned the man at the desk. "Just give me a minute to get you some visitors passes. Please stick them to the front of your jackets and keep them visible at all times. It probably wouldn't hurt if you kept your badges out as well. I can have someone from security escort you through the back hallways. According to the information I have here, the patient has been moved to pre-op. She is being prepped for surgery. I will have security escort you up to the waiting area if you like."

"Would it be possible to question the emergency room staff first?" Cecilia was thinking of how to better spend their time waiting for the results of the surgery and realized that sitting upstairs in a waiting area like the last couple of times was not going to work for her. She liked to keep herself busy and getting information while it is still fresh in peoples minds was something she learned early along in her career.

"Yes ma'am. Let me call an escort for you." He picked up the large, commercial phone resting on the simply decorated desk and within a few minutes there was an armed security guard at the desk. He acknowledged the officers with a military nod and indicated the direction, with a wave of his hand, to take the officers through the back hallway mazes. Paul, following the military influenced guard, went first. They walked through a door that required a pin, entered in a keypad, to the right of the knob. The guard was first through the door and walked with a brisk, authoritative pace that kept Paul in a state of hyperawareness. He was a fast walker but this was a step above his normal pace. It was as if the guard was leading them somewhere that required urgency. Paul glanced back at his partner, only to find her lagging behind the hurried pace. They turned a quick corner and he lost her altogether.

The emergency room was just like all the others they visited in the past. Machines whirring, the constant movement of bodies, and the drone of mixed voices indicating a busy part of the hospital. This can be 24 hours/7 days a week in a metropolitan hospital. It is quite in contrast to a ward floor, where patients are convalescing from various illnesses and diseases. Sometimes the solitude on these floors can be calming and reenergizing.

Cecilia made her way to the charge nurse's desk and asked to speak with the physician in charge of the "face case". The attending physician just happened to be behind the desk filling out the requisite paperwork for the admission and pre-operative forms for administration and accounting. She was a young lady, appearing to be just out of medical school, working on her internship. The nurse got her attention and explained that the detectives were there to get some information for their investigation. "Hello detectives, my name is Dr. Lewondowski. How may I help you?"

"Hello Dr., my name is detective Dower and this is my partner, Detective Sergeant Young. We wanted to ask you a few questions about the person that was brought here missing a face." Cecilia jumped right in.

"Well detectives, it really is a miracle that the young lady is alive. She came in, obviously, having her face excised and in bad shock. The curious part was that the wound appeared to be quite clean. Whoever put the bandages on knew the importance of keeping it clean and moist, so the bandages don't stick to the wound."

"Were there any burns or marks on her back?" Cecilia asked with the anticipation of a child waiting to go to Disney World.

"As a matter of fact, detective, there was some burning between the shoulder blades. As we were performing our detailed assessment, we came across what appeared to be a brand. Like what you might see on a horse or cow that belongs to a particular farm." the doctor expressed with a bit of surprise. She wasn't expecting to be asked a question about other marks on her body since the face was missing. It was the most obvious reason for the patient to be there and was the first time, in her career ,that she saw something so devastating to a patient.

"Thank you Dr. I think we have all we need for now. We know you are very busy and don't want to take up any more of your time. We may have more questions for you later, what is the best way to get in contact with you?"

"I just started a 72 hour rotation here at the hospital so I will be here for the next couple of days. The nurse's station can page me if I am not here in the emergency room. If it is later, I can be reached through the Chief of Emergency Service's office on the third floor."

"Thanks again doctor. Come on Paul, let's get up to the surgical floor to see how the patient is doing." Paul put away his small, expensive, moleskin notebook and they both met the security guard to be escorted up to the OR waiting area.

When the elevator doors opened, the security guard pointed to the right and told them the waiting area was the second door on the left. He was heading back down to the security office. He suggested they call if they needed anything else. Paul led the way to the waiting room, where there were several different families waiting for their loved ones to get out of surgery. None of the doctors or nurses were present and they both headed directly to the self serve coffee station to grab a cup. There was a crucifix on the wall above the coffee station. Cecilia said a little prayer for her and Paul to find the person responsible for all of these atrocities.

Sitting down across from one of the families present, Paul was thinking about the dread they all must be feeling as they sit their waiting to hear the fate of their family member. He tried to guess what they were in surgery for and how serious it was. It was a game he found himself playing every time he sat in one of these waiting rooms. The difference, he found, was that he wasn't emotionally attached to the situation. It wasn't one of his loved ones that he was waiting to hear about. He just sat there, stoically, sipping the extremely hot and bitter black coffee. He wasn't a man that physically displayed his emotions. For some reason he found himself staring at the people across the aisle. Why was this particular case affecting him this way?

Cecilia broke his thoughts as she plopped herself down in the chair next to his and started to speak. He was so deep in his thoughts at the moment that she sounded exactly like the teacher from the Charlie Brown cartoons he remembered when he was a child. That "whomp whomp whomp whomp!" was all he could make out. When he finally snapped out of it, Cecilia was asking him if he was listening to her. "Sorry Cel, I was jus thinkin bout the people over dere. I can't magine how tough it is to be sittin hir waitin for de doctor to come an tell you either thumbs up or down."

"Yeah, I hear ya. I was actually over at de coffee table praying to the crucifix. So what you thinkin bout all this? De third victim. No doubt the same MO. De brand in de back is de key!"

"I would say so. When we get outta here, les go back over to dat Garrett house in Brooklyn. We might have to sit on de house. A proper stakeout. If we lucky he'll come strollin in an we can scoop him up for questionin, right Cel?" Just then a doctor came into the room. He went right over to the family sitting across from them and said a few words. The relief in their eyes was all the detectives needed to know that their loved one was clear and going to be OK. No matter what the issue was, everything was going to be OK. The same couldn't be said for their victim. She might survive the surgery but was not going to be OK. She was going to suffer through a lifetime with a disfigured face. Cecilia couldn't help but feel sad for her. Paul sat there with a grin on his face and felt happy for the people across from him. He was sharing in their joy in hearing good news.

They were in the waiting room for about 2 hours when, finally, one of the nurses came in and asked them to follow her down the hall. One of the myriad offices on the floor was open and they were led into the room. It was a conservative office. Minimally furnished with a desk, comfortable chair, a few bookshelves, and two matching chairs across from the desk. As they entered, the doctor motioned to the chairs for them to have a seat. The nurse closed the door and there was a moment of silence as the doctor finished writing in the file on his desk. "Good evening detectives, my name is Dr. Shoenheim. The surgery went as expected. We had to take two grafts, each, from both of her thighs. We were able to successfully place the grafts on the open face. It really is going to be a waiting game now. Her prognosis is guarded at this point. We put her into an induced coma and a ventilator. It is the best way to manage both her pain and her recovery. I'm sorry but you won't be able to ask her any questions for the foreseeable future. Do you have any questions for me?"

"Thank you for the update Dr." Cecilia was livid at the idea that she sat there all that time, in the waiting room, to be told that she wouldn't be able question the faceless woman. " I do have a few questions but first I want to ask if there was anything questionable in her bloodwork?" Cecilia had so many questions but wanted to lead with this one. She was trying to see if there was any traces of chloroform in her blood when she was brought in. This was another similarity to the other two cases that could be used to tie things together.

"Other than what I would expect to see in a trauma of this kind, there was small amounts of chloroform found in her system. I can only surmise that this was how she was anesthetized during the procedure to remove her facial epidermis. Why do you ask?"

"Well we have two other victims that were also presented to the hospital with chloroform in their system. One had all of their fingers amputated and the other had both of his feet removed. So you can see how there might be a connection?" It wasn't so much a question but a way for Cecilia to tie all her efforts into this final moment. The question was rhetorical in nature. She knew that they were all tied together and wanted to hear all the details so she could assure herself about the right path. There was no doubt in her mind. She gave a quick smirk and looked over at her partner. Paul was happily listening to the conversation and taking notes in his moleskin. He, also, had not doubts about the similarities. He looked back at Cecilia and gave an open mouthed, full toothed smile. He knew they were getting close to the end of this case. His thoughts were interrupted as the Dr. spoke.

"This is very interesting. Please let me know if there is any way I can help in your case. I will be monitoring my patient for the next couple of weeks to ensure the healing. It is a delicate process when grafts are involved. Infection is a constant threat and can lead to septicemia if not treated immediately. Cases like this don't normally have a complete removal of the facial skin. I have only seen this in one other case that involved an automobile accident. The patient was put through the windshield. No seatbelt, I am told. The broken glass basically peeled away all the skin on one side of his face. This involves both sides."

"Did they fully recover?" Paul asked.

"As a matter of fact he did. He had a full recovery after about 10 plastic reconstructions. Although his case wasn't quite as severe as this one, the precautions are the same and the risks are the same. We will see in the next couple of weeks how the grafts take. She will have a long road ahead of her to reach full recovery. The possibility of losing some of her ability to provide specific facial features is high. I didn't see any obvious nerve damage but there could be small traumas that aren't immediately visible. We will know more when the ventilator is removed and she is out of the coma."

"Thank you again doctor. We don't want to take up any more of your valuable time. We will be in touch if we have any more questions. In the meantime we would appreciate any updates as well as a copy of the medical files when they are finished. *We need to start comparing with our other two cases and see if we can strengthen our theory.*"

"Have a good evening and I will have my office get in touch with any updates. As for the file, it should be ready for you sometime tomorrow. Again, I will have my secretary get a hold of you directly for the logistics." The detectives headed back to the Impala for the journey to the office. Neither one of them spoke as they thought about the case and how close they were getting to the answers they sought for the questions they had.

XX

Paul and Cecilia were sitting in the Impala just a few houses down from Garrett's. The sun was about to come up over the street and Cecilia gave Paul a jab in the ribs. She couldn't take another minute of his snoring. "Wake up Mr. Thang! De sun comin up. I don't know bout you but I needs to get out and stretch my legs. I ain't sat on a stakeout in a long time. Watched a lot of movies where they did it but it ain't the same as actually doin it."

"I'm starvin. Do we have anythin else in here to eat? Maybe we can slip out for a while and go grab a bite to eat. Is dere anythin open round here? How bout a diner? I could go for somethin heavy like meatloaf." His hoarse voice and putrid breath was the last straw for Cecilia.

"You gotta keep yo mouth turnt de other way, okay Mr.? I'm gonna punch you if ya look back over here wit dat stanky breath! Did you go to the bathroom in yo mouth?"

"You ain't no prize either Cel" he said with his head facing the passenger side window.

"Les just find somewheres up de strip where we can sit, eat, and collect ourselves. I'm bout to kill ya an we only been sittin in dis car overnight. How you live with yoself smellin like dat?"

"Jus drive de car Cel! I think dere a 24 hour pharmacy nearby in Brooklyn. I'll go in an get us a tube a toothpaste. Ain't there any mints in da glove box? How bout in yo door over der?"

"No, I sucked on the last of em las night while you was cutting down all dose trees. I'm surprised we ain't wake da neighbors wit all your snoring! You might need to go get dat checked out! They got machines to fix that bullshit!" She was starting to enjoy busting his balls after a night like that. She was irritated at the no show of their suspect.

"Alright, alright, enough! We been at it all night. Les jus git goin and come back to dis later." They put their seats back upright and headed towards Ritchie Highway.

Refreshed, fed, and not smelling like barnyard animals, they left the diner and headed back to Garrett's house. It was 1000a in the morning and most of the neighbors already left for work. There were a few people on their daily walk and the occasional person walking their dog to the park down the bottom of the hill. No movement at the house in the last 14 hours. Paul noticed one of the curtains moving on the second floor of the old cape cod. "Hey Cel, hand me the binos. I pretty sure I seen someone rustle the curtains in dat upper lef han window."

"Les go up and knock on de door. We might already be made. It kind a obvious dat we been sittin here on de side of de road all night. Anyone could a figured out dat we been watchin somethin round here. If he seen us den it won't matter noway." She was starting to worry about their exposure.

"Alright. How bout you stay here, in case he tries to slip out de back? I'll go up to de front door and knock. De house be covered dat way."

"Sound good! Be careful partner. Dis guy ain't playin with de same cards we is. You got yo pistol?"

"Always. Be back" He got out of the car, with authority, and strode across the street. He kept his gaze towards the side of the house as he made his way to the front. There was only one window on the ground floor on that side of the house and there wasn't any movement that he could see. Perhaps Garrett was barricaded on the second floor. Hiding from the world and his sins. Paul was determined to face this guy and get some answers. There seemed to be enough evidence to prove he was the suspect and they were some pretty heavy crimes.

As he approached the front steps, he took one last look up at the windows but there wasn't any movement. Maybe he was just seeing things? He knocked on the door while identifying himself as police. After about 20 seconds he attempted to knock on the door again. This time he placed his ear against the door, for a couple seconds, to see if he could hear any movement. There wasn't any glass in the door. It was just a heavy solid wood door, painted a navy blue. There was only a small peephole. Paul tried to look through it but all he saw was blurry bits of light and dark. There was a tool to reverse the focus but they didn't have one in the car. It wasn't a generally issued item for detectives. The SWAT team carried one around and he was wishing he had one at that moment. He gave it one more authoritative knock and stepped back off the stairs onto the grass. Not a sound or a visible movement. Heading back to the car he saw Cecilia looking at him with her shoulders up in an inquisitive pose, eyes wide opened. He mouthed over at her that there was nothing. She shook her head a couple times and motioned him back into the car. "Look, I need to go home and get some rest. How you feelin?"

"I could use some res too Cel. Les come back later, after supper and do dis gain. He bound to slip up and show himself. We can find another spot to sit and watch." They headed back to the office and decided to call it a day, agreeing to return that evening, rested and fed.

Upstairs in the dark room, Garrett was leaning against the exterior wall, underneath the window, with a view to the front yard. Glock in hand, against his forehead, and M4 Colt rifle leaning beside him, he was picturing the deep, dark jungle all around him. He occasionally had flashbacks like this and the detectives outside in the car, down the road, triggered another one. Although not diagnosed, officially, with PTSD, symptoms like this were a clear indication that he had some deeply rooted problems from his time in the service. He wasn't prone to paranoid delusions and knew that he was being stalked like prey by the authorities now. His greatest fears were confirmed when the loud knocking came at the front door earlier this morning. He had no problem going completely silent in stressful situations. He was ruminating over what led them to his front door. *Did I leave some evidence behind linking me to the malevolent souls I punished? Why are they knocking at my door?*

His mind went back to the jungle. The heat was enveloping. The darkness and silence was only broached by the screech of the monkeys in the trees. He was sweating from every single pore on his body. The BDUs he wore, Vietnam era tiger stripes, were completely soaked. Thankfully they were a modern material that helped wick some of the moisture away from his body but even that had its limits. His team members were all laying in their jungle bags 10 feet from each other, scattered on the canopy floor. Other than the monkey sounds and the occasional branch falling from the crowded trees above, the undergrowth was quiet. They received intelligence during one of their planned radio dispatches that a bounty was placed on their heads from the cartel. Mercenaries from all around were on search and kill missions for his team. A few of the surviving lab workers, mostly children, identified the unit to the cartel bosses. Enraged at the loss of so many labs and kilos of product, they decided to open the field to outside help. Professionals in the area of guerrilla warfare were called from all corners of the globe to find this group of people that were destroying their livelihoods. They were known as the "Dogs". "Uálace" in the local Yucana dialect. More specifically, they were short-eared jungle fox. The tribes in the area were afraid of them and knew the ferocity of the jungle dog. This was how they got their nom de guerre and it was a perfect fit.

Garrett and his team resorted to keeping lower profiles on the recommendation of their superiors. They took some time off, living among the jungle animals, sleeping where they could find protection. The hunters were being hunted. It was the first time in his career when he felt like he had some competition and his life was in danger. The mercenaries were a dangerous bunch and motivated by one thing. Money. The rumors surrounding their bounty reached into the millions per head. Literally, the bounty was only payable if a head was presented after removal from the body. It was a cringe worthy thought for him and his mates. What the mercenaries didn't know was they were also professionals. Years of training and field experience. They weren't going to allow a couple of hiccups get in the way of the mission. It turned into a counterintelligence operation for the time being.

Garret opened his eyes and realized he was still sitting in the dark, in his bedroom, with his weapons within arms reach. *I have been in this position before and will find a way out.* He kept a watch on the car and noticed that it was gone. *Did they give up for the day? This is my opportunity to get out.* He packed a bag with some clothes and his weapons. Heading downstairs he figured he would slip out the back door and hop the neighbor's fence.

He sat down at the dining room table and slipped back into the jungle. He and his team were in a cat and mouse game for their lives. Fortunately, they learned a few tricks along the way to throw off the pursuers. One thing they did was split the team in two groups. The first team would act as the bait to lure the mercenaries in. The second team was the ambush. It was unclear how many people were looking for them but they were sure they would hunt in groups. It would be suicide for a lone wolf to go after a unit of professional soldiers, especially this particular group of highly trained Green Berets.

In a deep ravine, the first group settled in for the night. Bags on the ground, they pretended to sleep. Group 2 took positions about 500 meters on the hillside. With night vision and thermal capabilities, they scanned the area for the stalkers. It was a couple of hours before the first few mercenaries were spotted coming along the ridge above the first group. They assumed they were also equipped with night vision and took the appropriate counter measures. Using the thick cover of the undergrowth and trees, they placed themselves to avoid the advantage of using optics to find them. Meanwhile, the first group was just laying out on the ground tucked in wherever they could find some comfort. As the stalkers approached, the second team started picking them off one by one. Using suppressed long rifles, they took advantage of the distance between the group members to pick them off one by one. The thermal scope helped define their prey and within 5 minutes, all their pursuers were out of commission. When the second group came off the mountain and met the first group, they were all fast asleep.

Garrett once again opened his eyes and was still sitting at the table in his dining area. He looked up at the clock and realized he had been there for almost an hour. One more look out the window and he slipped out the back door and across the neighbor's fence. He made his way to the back alley and towards the highway. He would walk across the street to Curtis Bay and head to his friend's house. The one that made the brand for him. Without revealing the whole situation, he was going to see if he could stay there for a couple nights while he worked on an escape plan.

Garrett spent the next couple of nights in Curtis Bay. He reached out to Kendall for a meeting to discuss the new events. They planned on a meeting at the pier at Fells Point. "Mr. Stemway, what is going on? I am hearing a lot of strange buzz going on in the city about a serial assaulter. Are they talking about you?"

"Listen Kendall, I've got a few things to tell you. First, I took care of your brother-in-law's situation. You won't have to worry about him anymore. Second, the police are sniffing around my home. They were knocking at my door yesterday and I had to play dead for a couple of hours. I don't know how they are on to me but it is really fucking with me. You haven't said anything to them, have you?"

"No way man! I wouldn't want to be implicated in any of this. I'm like the little boy that shit his pants in grade school. 'I don't smell nothin!' So they came to your house? That is some scary shit!"

"Yeah, tell me about it...I'm not saying they know we are colluding but if they approach you, just keep calm and deny everything. That little boy that shit his pants in school is going to pay off!" Just then, Garrett faded off for a few seconds as he pictured this humorous anecdote. It was a needed distraction amidst all the chaos that was now surrounding him. "Well I don't know how your going to tell your sister but you should leave out the details. Just let her know that anything that her husband was doing he isn't doing anymore. Just leave it at that."

"Will do. And thank you. Where should we go from here? I am really nervous now that the police are sniffing around." Kendall said with an anxious grin.

"Just lay low and we won't contact each other for a couple of weeks. That is the best way to see how bad things are. Just lay low and pretend nothing happened. Continue on with your life and work as usual and forget about me. That is the best advice I can give you for now. When the time is right and the coast appears clear, you will hear from me." Garrett started walking towards downtown Baltimore as Kendall slid off in the opposite direction. He was going to head over to his sister's house near Johns Hopkins and tell her the good news.

XXI

A couple of weeks went by and Garrett moved from one shitty motel to another along the outskirts of the city. Meanwhile, Kendall assured his sister that her marriage would be saved and she could stop worrying about her husband's infidelity. The turmoil seemed to quiet down as the detectives worked on other cases.

In the middle of the second week, Trish was taken out of the induced coma and the ventilator was removed. Her prognosis was improving but the damage to her face was irreparable. The doctors were able to keep the infections down while the grafts took a hold but she would need multiple cosmetic surgeries to rebuild her nose and the areas around her lips. The healing caused her skin to tighten around her mouth and it was difficult for her to talk. As soon as she was awakened, Dr. Shoenheim called the detectives. When they arrived the next day, Trish was up and sucking her lunch through a straw. She was on a strictly liquid diet to slowly transition to solid foods. She was fed through a nasogastric tube during her coma. "Ms. Kantwell, I am glad to see that you are recovering from this ordeal. May we ask you some questions?" Cecilia initiated the conversation as Trish sucked on the straw.

"I'll do my best but I really don't remember much." She replied as if her jaw were wired shut. The sounds were almost guttural but could be understood.

"What do you remember? How about anything you remember before the incident?" Cecilia was trying not to lead her into any made up answers. She wanted as much of the truth as she could remember.

"I remember watching some TV and then going upstairs to bed. It was a pretty typical night for me. Brush my teeth, put on my pajamas and crawl into bed. I really don't remember anything until I woke up with bloody bandages on my face. My back was killing me and I went to the mirror. I blacked out after that. I don't even know how I ended up in the hospital. I just remember waking up in this bed a couple days ago and wondering what happened." She started crying uncontrollably and the nurse came in to help her.

"I'm sorry detectives but Ms. Kantwell needs to get her rest. As you can imagine this is a delicate time for her. Please come back tomorrow." The nurse was insistent. It was her duty to protect her patient and the crying was only making her worse.

"I can understand that. Well we'll come back tomorrow Ms. Kantwell. I hope you will feel better then. Please try to remember any details. Sometimes the littlest thing can be a big help in figuring these things out. Anyway, come on Paul. Let's leave the lady to it." With that they both collected their things and headed back to the office. When they arrived there was a note on Paul's desk from another detective in the unit.

It said he had some information about their case and would meet him later for drinks. Paul didn't say anything to Cecilia because he knew how she felt about his drinking. He told her he was leaving for the day and would catch up with her tomorrow. On the way out he stopped at the other detectives desk and they both left together to go to the cop bar around the corner.

The Roost Bar was on the south side of the central police district station. Most of the drinkers there were cops, former police officers, or their wives. The decor in the bar reflected the patronage. Patches adorned the walls from police departments and military units all over the country. Flags were hanging from just about every square inch of the ceiling, reflecting anything from the police, to different sports teams. The testosterone in the room was enough to run the average person out and never come back. That included the testosterone that exuded from the female cops. Constant bickering and finger pointing was common and the conversations were usually about the days business.

Paul and his colleague found a corner table and ordered 2 boilermakers. When the drinks arrived, Paul's friend started right in to the meat and potatoes of the meeting. "Paul, listen man. I think I saw your suspect today in Fells Point. Me and the boys were runnin a stolen car thing in the area. I remember the fliers you and Cel put around the office. I can't be positive but I think it was him. You remember the old station near the pier? Well I saw that guy there talking to one of the newspaper people. They weren't there long but I'm pretty sure the guy was a match."

"Well that some great news! We been sittin on that guy house for a while and ain't turned up a thing. We thought he might a lef town. There ain't been any activity in a couple weeks. Not since dat girl got her face removed. We confirmed it was related to de other two. We think they related because of the brand dey all three victims have on dey backs. So you think this our guy? Cel gonna be beside herself. And you say he was wit de guy dat writes for the Sun?"

"I think so man. Cheers!" They both dropped in the shot of bourbon, watched the foam and alcohols mix, and chugged the boilermakers until they were empty. "Les git one more Paul. Then I gots ta get home to da wife!"

"Sound like a plan. I think I better go back to de office an see if Cel still der. She wanna hear this right away." They both repeated the ritual of the Boilermaker and headed out. When Paul arrived back at the office, Cecilia had already left for the day. He went to his desk and dialed her cell. "Hey Cel. Have I got some news for you…"

On the other side of the city, Kendall was knocking at his sister's house. When she answered, he said he wanted to give her some good news. "Are the kids around? Listen sis, you don't need to worry about Tom anymore. I told you I would take care of it and it is done. Have you noticed Tom any different lately?"

"As a matter of fact, he has been slinking around the house in a depressed mood but at least he is here and not out. The kids are sleeping by now. Tom is up in the bedroom watching some bullshit on TV. Probably the news. Are you staying?"

"No, sorry. I want to get back to the apartment. I still have some writing to finish for tomorrows run. Well, I just wanted to let you know that things are taken care of on that front. I would suspect that Tom will get over it soon and you guys can work on your marriage for the kids sake. Anyhoo...I'll leave you to it then."

"Thanks again Kendall. I love you and think about you often. I'll let the kids know you missed them. They love their uncle and miss seeing him. You should come around for dinner one day next week."

"I'll let you know when I have some free time and we can get together. I would like to see the kids too. Well, love you!" He went out the front door and headed for home. He smiled on his way as he thought about how happy he made his sister and how much better her life would get now that she didn't have to worry about Tom running around.

Cecilia made it in early the next morning and waited for Paul. She could tell he was drinking when he called last night. Something in the timbre of his voice changes when he has a few drinks. She started researching the journalist that he spoke about. His name was Kendall Firth and he worked for the Baltimore Sun on the police blotter. He was employed there for the last couple years and lived in a small apartment in the Mount Vernon neighborhood. When Paul came in she already had an address and they headed for the Impala. "You think he be at home?" Paul asked with the gruff voice that follows a hangover.

"I don't know Mr. Thang but you need to get some coffee in you" Cecilia replied admonishingly.

"Les just make a quick stop at the mart round the corner. I'll be fine Cel. It might not be ideal but I got us some information. You know how he like to drink after work. Besides, I'm the one that had to take the hit for the team. You think I enjoy feeling like this every morning?"

"I don't know but it seem like it becomin every day now. Anyway, anyway les stick to the job now!" She expressed her disgust by waving her hands around with the index finger pointing straight at him as if to shush him up. She didn't want to hear any of his bullshit this morning. She was laser focused on getting the case closed and moving up the career ladder.

"Ok, Ok, I know. Les jus get to de house and see if he dere. I can get some coffee when we get back. They any of dose mints in de glove box? De ones we got de other day when we was staking out de house in Brooklyn?" She opened the box and got out the tin of Altoids. The spearmint smell was so strong it creeped up her nose before she even opened the box. Paul reached in past the white cellophane paper and grabbed three of them. He liked to swirl them around his mouth without biting them until they melted into nothing.

The apartment was only about 10 minutes from the district office in early morning Baltimore City traffic. They had to park about a block away because the row homes don't have garages. The entire neighborhood is street parking, permit only. They had the official city license plate on their undercover Impala so it didn't apply. Walking to the apartment building, Paul noticed what a nice clean neighborhood it was compared to some on the west side of the city. Although most of the high rise tenement buildings are gone, there are still some shady government housing projects that reminded him of where he grew up. He admired how the cobblestones seemed so perfectly set into the street. The pavers on the sidewalk amazed him considering they were just sitting on a bed of sand and crushed stone. Even the elegant stairways and formed concrete handrails made this neighborhood appear very pricey. He wondered how a journalist working at the Baltimore Sun could afford to live in a neighborhood like this.

Climbing the stone steps to the flagstone façade building, Paul couldn't help but wish he were coming home to his own house. Cecilia looked at the information placard on the wall adjacent to the door and pushed the button next to the name "Firth". They could hear the buzzing of the bell. There were only three floors to the building and there were six apartments. Two on each floor. One facing the street and one looking out into the Old Town neighborhood. Kendall's apartment was 2B. Cecilia assumed that meant his was facing Old Town in the back of the building. They waited for approximately 30 seconds and there was no answer. She pressed the button to the buzzing of the bell again. This time she left her finger on the buzzer for a few seconds longer. The scratchy speaker came alive and the voice on the other end asked, "Who is it?"

"Its detectives Dower and Young from the Baltimore City Police. Can we speak, please?"

"Just a minute, I'll be right down." He tried to hide the panic that was rising from his testicles to his throat. The terror immediately took over his mind and the tried and true, fight or flight response kicked in. He didn't want them to come into his apartment and was relieved that the words coming out of his mouth weren't come on up. Instead, he heard himself say he would be right down as if it was an out of body experience. Garrett had warned him that the police were sniffing around his house but he couldn't figure out how they wound up on his front stoop. He felt like his skin was going to crawl right off his body, open the window, and fly away. That is what he wanted to do anyway. After that first few seconds of shock, Kendall started to rationalize their being here. He reached for his jacket and keys. On the coat rack was his computer bag and he pulled that over his shoulder. The whole time the menial tasks were going on outside his body, his mind was trying to figure out a plan to tell the police. He figured the best story was that he needed to get to the office to post his blotter for the evening run of the paper. He locked the apartment and headed down the stairs. Opening the front door, he saw standing there, an enormous black man in a suit and a plump black woman that appeared to be wearing a curly wig. "Good morning detectives, I was just on my way out to work. How can I help you?"

"We just need a few moments of your time. Can we speak upstairs?"

"No, I really need to get to work. I have a deadline for the evening run and I can't miss it. Is it something related to my column? I can easily print a retraction if I made a mistake."

"No Mr. Firth, it pertains to several cases were are working on. Do you know a Mr. Garrett Kunter? We believe you met with him yesterday in Fells Point."

"I am not sure I know who you are talking about. That name is not familiar to me." The detectives didn't know that Kendall was introduced to an alias. Roger Stemway. That was the name he knew. Garrett had been very careful about not using his real name in the interaction. It was about this time that Cecilia reached into her jacket pocket and pulled out the picture of Garrett that they found in the database. It was an old Army photo from his graduation from the medical school.

"This is the man we are speaking of. Take a look at it Mr. Firth. Are you certain that you don't know this person? We have an eyewitness that says you were talking with this gentleman at the pier in Fells Point."

"Yes, this was the man I spoke with briefly yesterday but his name isn't Garrett whatever you said. He told me his name was Roger Stemway." He couldn't believe he said yes. He was starting to panic and was sure they could tell.

"May we know what the nature of your conversation was?" This question stunned the poor deer. The headlights were getting brighter, larger, and focused directly into his eyes. Kendall was scrambling what was left of his brains, trying to come up with a believable answer to this question. All he could come up with was, "Yeah, he was asking me about Fleet Week. He wanted to know when it was and how many ships usually came. He wanted to know if there were any foreign ships there during the week. He said he was a sailor and enjoyed looking at other ships." He was mortified at the bullshit that came out of his mouth. He wasn't even sure if he could remember it all because of the shock. *If you believe it then it must be true*, he thought to himself.

"That is interesting. So you just bumped into this man and he wanted to know about Fleet Week, huh? So when is Fleet Week?" Another punch in the face. The level of paranoia now flowing through his mind was becoming unbearable. *Deny, deny, deny.* That was what Garrett told him. "I have no idea. It has been a while since I've been but I know it happens at the harbor during the summer." Yes, he thought, take that you pigs!

"Well we know you need to go. We'll be in touch if we have any more questions. In the meantime, please think more about your conversation with this man you know as Roger Stemway. I am not so sure he is who he says he is." The detectives headed down the paved sidewalk back to the Impala. Kendall stood there frozen for a couple of minutes and realized he was looking awfully guilty standing there like that. He turned the opposite way and started walking down the street. It was the wrong direction for work so he popped into the corner mart and went to the back aisle to take a few deep breaths. It was then he noticed that both of his hands were shaking uncontrollably. Adrenaline was coursing through his body. He needed to call Roger right away and let him know the cops were on to both of them now.

"What the HELL are you calling me for on this phone? I told you we need to keep our distance until the smoke clears."

"Listen Roger, the cops came to my apartment for fuck sake!"

"What did you tell them you little weasel?"

"I didn't tell them anything! They say that someone saw us together that day in Fells Point. They were asking me what we talked about. I told them we just bumped into each other and you were asking me about Fleet Week."

"Fucking Fleet Week? What the Hell!" Garrett got real quiet for a minute while he thought about the next move.

"They also said that your name wasn't Roger Stemway. They said your name was Garrett Kunter. Is that true?" Garrett was as quiet as a mouse on the other end of the line. He was still trying to process all the new information that he was getting. "Well...I thought we were on the same page here. They are telling me to watch out for you. The black lady told me that you weren't who you say you are. How am I supposed to take that?"

"Fuck them. They are just trying to rattle your cage, man!" Garrett replied as he deflected the question about his name. "My name is Roger Stemway. They can go to HELL! Why would you believe them?"

"Well they came to my fucking apartment Roger! How the fuck am I supposed to react? I have never had the police come looking for me at my home! Have you? I mean anytime before this?"

"Look man. They are just barking up a tree and looking for the reaction." He was thinking of the dogs that hunt for mountain lions. They just chase the cat up the tree and sit around the base barking. Meanwhile the cat just looks down from above and waits for them to either get bored and leave or for another escape route in the trees next door. "Just keep your head on. You did the right thing telling them I was a stranger asking for directions or whatever. It was a great knee jerk answer. Just let's cool our guns here for a minute while I think."

"Well you just keep on thinking man. I am heading to the nearest bar to get a drink and calm the fuck down. My hands haven't fully stopped shaking since they left and I need some time to decompress. Just call me when you decide where we go from here."

"Alright! Keep the phone close. I'll send you a text. I won't call next time. If the phone rings, it isn't me. Know and remember that. If you don't get a text from me then just hold fast. Gotta go!" Garrett hung up the phone and stood there, eyes wide open, in a state of shock. He couldn't believe that this was coming down on him already. And so fucking fast! He had to figure out how to diffuse the situation. *Maybe I should leave town. Maybe its better if I just disappear and start over in another town.* It was the first time, in a long time, that he was indecisive. He was more shocked about his inability to make a command decision than the fact that he was being hunted...again.

Back at the Central District office, Cecilia and Paul were going over the files, again, in the conference room. They set up a board with pictures of Kendall, Garrett, and the three known victims. There were various index cards with investigative information on each subject tacked to the board underneath the pictures. Fingerprints, pictures of the gruesome amputations, and textual information all scattered and attached with push pins. Cecilia got up and started to arrange the index cards according to each separate case. She took all three photos of the brands and aligned them in a linear, horizontal fashion just underneath the victims pictures. Each corresponding to the appropriate body. "Paul, dis de best piece of corroborative evidence we have dat link dese three victims together. Ain't dis de point we can call this a serial case?"

"I think so Cel. It take three cases tied together to consider a murderer a serial killer, right?"

"Dat what I heard too. So...we got three cases hir an each one has de exact same brand. Dis sicko want to mark his victims. Did we get back de info bout de brand? Do it match anything in the databases?"

"I don't think so Cel. I don't think we got back anythin yet. When you see dem next to each other, dere really ain't no denyin de similarities, is dere?"

"Sure nuff ain't" Cecilia paused for a minute as she rearranged some more cards on the board. She put the fingerprint cards underneath the two victims that had a match. Scott Finlay and Lamar Jenkins were no doubt matches, both in branding as well as fingerprint evidence. There wasn't any fingerprint evidence for Trish's case yet. "Hey Paul, we shook de tree dis mornin with that Kendall. Did ya notice he seem nervous and avoidin us?"

"Sure did! Matter of fact, I notice dat he ain't goin in the right direction for the Sun offices when he left. He woulda gone with us towards de car. It don't mean nothin but he did say he was late an on de way to work. Member?"

"I sure do Mr. Smarty Pants. I also think he got on de phone with our suspect an probly warnt him dat we snoopin round. We ain't got a warrant to bug de phones but we can go sit on Garrett house an see what fall from de tree. Wadda ya think?"

"I gotta tell ya Cel, I jus don't like lookin at a bunch a papers and pictures. I wanna get into de action. Les go now an sit on de house for a while and see he turn up. I bet he get some rabbit in him and try to run. If he do, he gonna need some stuff from home, don't ya think?"

"Sure nuff. Les go now!" They both headed down the stairs to the parking lot. They have spent a lot of time in the Impala and were looking forward to making some progress with Garrett.

When they arrived at the house, it looked the same as the last time they were there. Shades were drawn. The house looked deserted. They were determined to get a read on the situation this time. If they came up empty they were going to canvass some of the close neighbors. They decided earlier to leave them alone so not to spook Garrett, in case he was close with his neighbors. Paul and Cecilia, feeling like they were getting close, decided to change tactics and start putting the pressure on him. If the neighbors were privy to some inside information, maybe they would be motivated to cooperate with the police.

A couple of hours passed and Paul noticed a light come through a small slit in the upstairs window he was watching the last time they were there. He was sure there wasn't a light before. "Hey Cel, take a look at de light comin from dat small crack in de shade. Upstairs lef window." He roused her from the nap she was taking while he kept watch.

"Yeah, I sees it." she said as she rubbed her eyes. "Les not waste any time. I'll go to de front door myself, incognito (she meant without her badge out) and see I can get him to answer de door. You go round to de back porch an cover it in case he decide to make a break for it. I'll identify myself after he open de door. We gonna have to get on the grey side of de line for this to work. Les get on this." They both got out of the car at the same time, splitting towards their respective posts. Cecilia began a light knocking on the door. The doorbell wasn't working and looked like it was original with the house. She waited patiently for a minute and knocked on the door. She heard the sound of a lock being turned and the door opening, she got herself into work mode and as soon as the door opened she asked, "Are you Garrett Kunter?" He attempted to shut the door on her but she put her foot in the jamb. She let out a quick howl as the door pinched her foot. She removed her firearm and pointed it in the crack of the door. "Open this fuckin door right now mother fucker! You just crushed my foot and I ain't in the mood!" she exclaimed with the authority that only a pissed off detective can provide.

"Fuck You!" Garrett shouted back, "This is my house!"

"You better open this door or I'm gonna shoot you motherfucker!" By that time Paul had heard the commotion and was already through the back door and into the house. They didn't have a warrant but decided that they had reasonable cause for a breech and arrest. There was no standoff. Garrett knew they got the drop on him. He was upstairs packing a bag to get out of town and they had him. He didn't even have the Glock. He assumed it was a religious fanatic at the door trying to sell Jesus or something. Paul got him cuffed and they called for a patrol car to come and bring him downtown for a battery of questions.

As the patrol car pulled away, Cecilia turned to Paul and he immediately knew the look. "We headin to de Sun now, ain't we? We gonna pick up dat boy Kendall and bring him in too?"

"Paul, you and I been partners long nuff now. You read me like a book. Yes sir, Mr. Thang! Now get yo ass in de car an take me to de Sun." They both got in the Impala and headed back downtown to go pick up Kendall at his job. They were happy to have them both together for questioning. It is a wonderful tactic to separate two alleged suspects and see how different or the same their stories can be. Especially if they are taken by surprise and don't have any time to get their information straight. Only time would tell and these two detectives were familiar with the "Good Cop, Bad Cop" routine.

XXII

The interrogation room wasn't what he expected. It reminded him of one of those closet offices like in that movie, "Office Space", where the guy was relegated to a basement storage room. There was a desk/table with two chairs on one side and one more on the opposite. There was a camera in the far corner where the ceiling met the wall. But the most influential aspect was the temperature. The room felt like it was about 35 degrees Fahrenheit. It was fucking freezing. Garrett was trying to channel his time in SEER training. He tucked his arms inside his shirt, sans jacket, and hugged his legs together to try and keep warm. This wasn't his first foray into an interrogation and he was sure he went through far worse in his training. He was determined to hold his line. *What is the worst they can do to me that I haven't already experienced. They aren't going to strip me naked, they aren't going to water board me. If I can keep my mouth shut, maybe I can get out of this and out of town.*

Just like his training, he wasn't able to keep track of time. There was no clock on the wall. They used daylight bulbs, the highest candle watt bulbs on the market, to light the room. It was hard to try and get any rest. Between the near freezing temperature and the bright lights, the normal perpetrator would be conditioned to quit and give up whatever information the interrogators asked for. Garrett, obviously, did not fit this profile. He was a professional soldier with DOD training in the arts of interrogation well above the pay grade of a couple of city detectives. Paul and Cecilia were aware of this and decided that a different approach might bring this to a close.

Having an alleged accomplice in an adjacent room was perfect for the "He said, He said" scenario that they were expecting from the pair. They also knew that their best chance at a crack was with Kendall. He was young, unfamiliar with interrogations, and genuinely naive in the world. They decided to get to Garrett first and start getting him into scramble mode. Then they would hit Kendall with Bad Cop right off the bat. Continuing a back and forth campaign until one of them gave up. Their bets were both on Kendall. They knew he was the weak link. He was going to be their best way through this. They wanted to be able to bring something to him from Garrett so they figured it was best to start with him and get some kind of statement that would rattle Kendall's emotional cage.

"Good afternoon Mr. Kunter. Or is it Mr. Stemway? We seem to have both names here. Is there a particular way you would like to be addressed?" Garrett just looked down at the table. His hands were stuffed in his shirt and he was gripping the belt loop of his pants. "Nothing? Well my colleague and I are familiar with your background and would expect nothing less than the silent treatment in the beginning. Just know that we have your partner in the next room and we are convinced he is a pussy! He is gonna take a couple of minutes to work on and I'm convinced he will sing like a bird. Is there anything you want us to pass along to him when we leave you here? I am sure this isn't the worse environment you have been in. I am also sure you are aware that we have a 48 hour hold policy while we conduct our questioning. Well if you don't have anything to pass on to your colleague, we'll leave you to it. Come on Paul." He was standing in the back corner of the small room giving the "fuck you" stare to Garrett the whole time. It turns out that Cecilia was going to play the Good Cop for the meantime. It is always the silent one that you have to watch out for. Paul followed Cecilia out of the room, staring into Garrett's eyes the entire time. Garrett gave him a wink as he left and it threw him off his track for a second. "Do you know that SOB just gave me a wink. I mean what kind of a person smiles and winks when he is in the corner?"

"Don't worry bout him. He ain't de one dat gonna to give it all up for us. Les go see de other one. He weak and timid. I guess we gonna get a mountain of information from him. You wanna play the good one dis time?"

"No thank you. I'm perfectly happy standin in de back with my arms crossed, starin. You got dis. I'll jump in if you need me but I think I'm better at keepin quiet. I like fosterin paranoia and fear. You do you Cel. I got your back. Les go turn dis guy inside out."

Kendall's room was the same as the one that Garrett was in. It was so cold that he sat in the chair shivering. He also had his arms inside his shirt trying to keep as much body heat to himself as possible. The reality was, it wasn't working. He knew he wasn't going to last long and was already trying to work out what to say to keep himself clean. *Oh who am I fooling? They must know something or I wouldn't be here. Just stick to the story you already created. Deny, deny, deny.* The words were creeping back into his subconscious. "Hello, again, Mr. Firth. Sorry for the disruption at your office but we had a few more questions to ask you about your friend. Oh, I forgot, he wasn't your friend. He was just someone you bumped into that wanted to know about Fleet Week at Inner Harbor. Is that still your story?" Kendall almost shit himself. They obviously knew more than they were letting on. Just the way they phrased the questions was enough to let him know that they knew he was lying. *Oh shit! What the hell am I going to say now? Deny, deny, deny.* It was becoming a mantra; a permanent part of his brain patterns. "I don't know what you're getting at detective. Are you still trying to squeeze me for answering a stranger's question? I never met that guy before in my life. He said he was a sailor and was interested in the ships that come into the harbor for Fleet Week. That is all I know. What else do you think I can give you?"

"One of our undercover detectives was following you and saw you both shake hands when you first met. Is that a normal way that you meet strangers you bump into? Do you shake hands when someone is looking for directions?" She said that to illicit a response.

It is an interrogative technique that has served her well over the years. Being confrontational is almost a prerequisite to good questioning in a captive environment. Sometimes, based on the person's will, this simple tool can lead to an immediate confession.

Kendall sat across the table with a blank stare. He was still in shock that he was in the police station not more than 24 hours after engaging with these officers at his home. It was an indication to him of the urgency of the situation. They were even closer to the answers they needed now then 12 hours ago. He entertained the idea that they already knew all the answers to the questions. They were asking them with such confidence. *Who the fuck do they think they are? How could they possibly know anything about a connection between me and Roger? Why do they say his name isn't Roger? When I approached him about this he didn't answer me. Are they telling me the truth?* He started to have the usual moments of doubt. *I need to keep it together. They are on to me now. Should I just come out and tell them? What do they know?* He was beginning to go crazy. He was approaching the crossroad between lucidity and fantasy.

"What the hell are you talking about? Is it against the law to shake a person's hand? So what if I shook his hand. Not that I would remember such a little thing. I shake a lot of people's hands. I can't believe that is what you brought me in here for. What is it about this guy that you think I am involved? Has he done something wrong? Why isn't anyone giving me the answers to my questions?" It was just then that he realized he was going too far. He was allowing his emotions to take him to an angry place. *The detectives will know that they are getting to me. Calm the fuck down asswipe! Just let them keep thinking whatever they want. They can't prove anything. Deny, deny, deny.* If there was one thing he wanted to keep going on in his mind it was to deny everything. Just the way that Roger told him to.

"We are gonna let you sit here and think some more about how you want to answer the questions we have. In the meantime, we have your stranger in the next room. Perhaps he has the same story or perhaps he has a different one. The next few minutes may determine the rest of your civilian life Mr. Firth. I hope that you will take this time to reflect on why and how you arrived here." The two detectives left the room and walked to their cubicles. They wanted Kendall to sit and percolate on the information that they gave him. It was apparent that he was affected by the questions they were asking. Simple questions about shaking someone's hand.

In the grand scheme of things this was a little event but the implications that it implied would elicit a strong feeling in someone that was guilty of something. That was their thought process anyway. It was just a matter of time and pressure, much like the forming of a diamond, before the results of their investigation would come to an end. They knew they were close to getting the answers they wanted to close the case. The two suspects they had in the interrogation rooms would provide those answers given the right application of force.

Garrett was in the next room, unaware of the pressure that was being applied to Kendall. He was focusing on his own particular set of circumstances and knew that his time there was short. There was a limit to what they could do to him. If he could just survive the next 48 hours, without breaking, he had a chance of walking out of there. Deep in the recesses of his mind he was concerned with Kendall and his ability to hold out against the persistent questioning that usually accompanied a hold like this. Kendall was a civilian with little to no understanding or training in counterintelligence.

Interrogators have a penchant for asking the same questions over and over. They will change a word or small aspect of the question to try and throw the suspect off. It is, essentially, the same question. This repetition is also an emotional attack meant to create chaos internally in the suspect. Self doubt is the enemy here and the sharks take advantage of the blood in the water. Any false attack against him, his family, or professional life would be an immediate break in his will. This break was a sure way for him to spill the proverbial beans, which included his interactions with Garrett.

One thing he knew that was going for him was the alias Roger Stemway. It is the only name that Kendall knows to go by and any other name they give him will only confuse him. On the other hand, it is not above the government to falsify information in order to get what they want. It wouldn't be a stretch for them to show Kendall his service record, which isn't fake documentation at all, and convince him that he was dealing with a completely different person that has lied to him. If he would lie to him about that then what else would he lie about. He was also an accomplice. A willing accomplice, especially in the case of his sister's husband and mistress. Kendall wasn't even sure if the detectives were aware of the connection but he didn't want that to get out. He would do whatever it took to ensure his innocence in all cases but especially the case that involved his family.

The detectives came into the room and Garrett was seated behind the desk, laying his head on the table. When they came in he lifted his head and looked at both of them. With a casual yawn, he laid his head back on the table and ignored them.

"Mr. Kunter. We just had a chat with someone you are familiar with. Do you know a Mr. Kendall Firth? He definitely knows you. We understand that you know each other enough to greet with a handshake. Does that sound accurate to you Mr. Stemway? Or is it Mr. Kunter? We still haven't figured out which name you go by. Apparently, Mr. Firth is familiar with you as Roger Stemway. According to the files we have here from your military jacket, your name is Garrett Kunter. You were retired from service about a year ago, after what can only be described as a colorful career. A lot of what we have here is redacted, which leads us to believe that you are a special person within the community. Would you care to share any light on Mr. Firth and his involvement in your extracurricular activities?"

Garrett didn't even lift his head off the table. It was about this time that Detective Young walked over to the table and with a crisp open hand, slapped the surface of the metal table with all his might. The sound was so loud and the vibration it created on the table caused Garrett's head to bounce twice on the hard metal surface. With a contemptuous smirk, he lifted his head and stared directly into Paul's eyes.

A moment of silence passed before detective Dower spoke, "Mr. Kunter, we have an abundance of evidence, including fingerprints from the scenes of the crimes, that point the finger directly at you. How do you think you were brought to our attention? Do you think we arbitrarily bring people here to spend our afternoons chasing our tails? It might help if you were to acknowledge us a bit. The clock is ticking and we are getting closer to securing our case against you. Right this minute one of our colleagues is procuring a warrant to search your house and car. I would imagine we will find a metal brand that will confidently link you to the cases we are currently working on. Do you have anything to say about that?"

"Go suck a bag of dicks lady!" It was the first time he said anything meaningful to the detectives. It was abusive and uncalled for but it was a reaction. It was something. Cecilia was hoping to elicit something and a big smile crossed her face when she was able to get some words out. It didn't phase her a bit that they were combative. It was something. She was forming a small crack in his unbreakable exterior. She knew if they kept poking they would eventually be able to get a crowbar in there and open him up. He had been in the central district office now for 12 hours. They still had plenty of time to get the evidence they needed to bury this guy.

Cecilia called for the officers to take him across the street to a holding cell. They were going to hold him for the entire 48 hours they were legally allowed to during an investigation. They came in and approached him. When they grabbed his arms to lift him up he, again, gave the stare of defiance. Neither of the two officers gave it a thought and directed him out of the room and down the hall.

There was a covered bridge that led from the central district offices to the booking and intake center. It was the first stop on the way to the penitentiary and some of the convicts were held there for months awaiting a trial date. Without bail it can be a long wait for a trial. The system is always clogged with cases and a speedy trial, as guaranteed in the constitution, is always up for interpretation. Garrett, reluctantly, went with the officers across the bridge and found himself in one of the many holding cells typical of a booking institution. A stainless steel sink and toilet combination was bolted to the wall in the corner and the accommodations consisted of a nice overly conditioned room with a concrete bench for a bed. After they removed his handcuffs, he went over to the bench, laid down, and fell immediately into a deep and relaxed sleep.

Back at the offices, Kendall was still being held in the interrogation room. The detectives were giving him an opportunity to think about the answers he was giving concerning his relationship with Garrett. He had some time to think in that cold room and came to the conclusion that it was better to save himself than spend any time in a jail cell for someone that he really didn't know. The fact that the detectives were adamant about his name being Garrett and not Roger was leaving an incredible rift of doubt in his psyche. He spent the time alone debating the pros and cons of spilling the beans. He decided to see what they were offering, in terms of immunity, for the information they wanted. He knew part of the bargain would include testifying in court with Garrett sitting across the room from him. It would certainly be the most difficult thing he will ever do in his life. After what felt like hours of freezing temperatures and lonely contemplation, the detectives finally entered the room. "Well

Kendall, may I call you Kendall? Have you had some time to think about your position? Do you think you can start telling us the truth?" It was then that he pulled himself up to the table and placed his hands in front of him.

"May I please have some water or perhaps a cup of coffee? Actually, can I have both? I have spent some time thinking about this and before I go into any details I want some assurances from you. I want to know if you are able to provide any immunity here for me."

"I have to be honest here Mr. Firth. I need to hear what you have to say first. If what you have to offer is useful and you aren't complicit in the actual crimes, then there is a possibility that I will be able to help you with that. We have a close relationship with the prosecutor's office and the DA will certainly entertain terms if they are appropriate. Do you have anything valuable to relay about what happened here?" Cecilia almost couldn't contain herself after this exchange.

"First, let me say that I am taking a huge leap of faith by telling you this without any assurances. I want that on the record. Second, I don't want to involve anyone else in this. It is between myself and Mr. Stemway...or rather Mr. Kunter. I think you are aware that I was introduced to him with the name Roger Stemway. He made first contact with me on the phone. He knew that I was the writer for the police blotter column in the Baltimore Sun paper. My name is at the bottom of the column and I can only surmise that he called the office looking for me. He said he wanted to meet to discuss some of the cases that I included a few months ago. Our first meeting was at a coffee house downtown. He wanted some information about my column. He asked that I give him first dibs at my articles before they are published. In his words he wanted to clean up the neighborhood of all the filthy people. I guess you could say he was an idealist. He said he was from Baltimore and was sad at the way there was such terrible people running around committing crimes against their own communities."

"So you met him in a coffee house and he went directly into the idea that he was going to be a sort of vigilante?"

"Yes. That is pretty much exactly how it went down. The second meeting we had was in a bar, which I can tell you he was not so happy about. He thought the bar was a dive and we could have met somewhere a bit more congested and noisy."

"What was he looking for this time?"

"I had a lead on a criminal that was released after having beaten a woman to near death near Patterson Park. He was going to take care of that piece of shit and make sure he couldn't do that to an innocent member of society again. It was a short meeting. He said he would be in touch and that was it." Kendall hesitated after telling about this meeting. He knew the only real information left to divulge was about his sister and her husband. He wasn't sure if he wanted to include himself in all this.

"Kendall, there is another case that just appeared in the last week. A woman was brought to the hospital with her face removed. She had some markings on her body that were consistent with the other two victims. Do you have anything to say about that?" Cecilia was happy with the results so far but wanted to see how much he knew about this victim. She could tell he was receding back into himself and avoiding any answers about this.

"We are convinced that all three of these victim cases are related. It would be helpful to our case if you could provide any insight on this." She figured she would make one more plea to him before she had him removed to a holding cell across the street. "Mr. Firth, it would really help both of our plights if you would just come out and tell us what happened in this situation." Kendall lowered his head to the table and appeared to check out. "Officers...could you please escort Mr. Firth across the street to a holding cell. We will be back tomorrow for more questions." The officers took Kendall across the bridge to a separate cell from Garrett for the night. It was important to keep them separated until the questioning was completed.

The next morning the warrant came back from the courthouse. It was sitting on Paul's desk when he arrived. "Hey Cel, take a look at dis. Our Wonka Golden Ticket has arrived. Les get a team together and head over to dis guy house."

"Sound good Mr. Thang! I wanna bring someone from de CSI as well." Once again, they headed for the Impala to gather the evidence that would put this criminal away for the rest of his life. He was uncomfortably sitting in the bull pen at central booking. Since he didn't want to talk, they were going to find something that would give him a bit more motivation to tell them more. If they found what they were looking for he was going to be charged. They just hoped they could find that smoking gun in the next 24 hours.

The CSI team, in conjunction with detectives Young and Dower took the next 18 or so hours searching every nook and cranny of the Brooklyn Park home of Garrett Kunter. Other than some fingerprints, to verify the ones they already had, there was nothing. It wasn't until they entered the detached garage and opened the trunk of his car that they found what they were looking for. After searching, their greatest wish was granted. In the trunk, they found the day bag that contained a bottle of chloroform, an old rag, duct tape, a plumber's torch, and the metal brand he used to mark the three victims in the back. It was a triumph. They both gave a fist bump with the rest of the team and loaded up the evidence. What appeared to be a complete loss turned out to be a victory in the highest way. This was the piece of evidence they needed to ensure the conviction. The "smoking gun". Cecilia was on the phone with the prosecutor's office when Paul noticed her face change. She went from all smiles to look of intense pain. "What up Cel?"

"Thank you for the update. I'll let the team know. Well Paul, it look like we took too long. They had to let him go. Apparently we outworked our 48 hour window. He was released about 20 minutes ago."

Paul was immediately on the phone with his colleague in the vice squad. "Hey man. They jus released one our suspects from central. You think you could keep a tail on him?... Yeah, his name Garrett Kunter. White male, medium build, bout 6 feet. Last seen wearin a red t-shirt, jeans, an a older jacket. I think it was light grey. Please let me know if you catch up wit him. And do follow him til Cel and I can catch up. We got de evidence we need to charge but our time ran out holding him...Great man! I owe you one!"

He hung up the phone and walked over to the car where Cecilia was staring at the ground and shaking her head. "Dis was our chance Paul. We gonna close one a de most important cases of our careers an he slipped through de crack. What we gonna do now? He probly already on his way to bumfuck Egypt."

"No ma'am. I jus got off de phone wit my man in vice. I told him who we after an he jus got released. He said he gonna take a look and try to catch up wit him. He know not to engage but will call me if he find him. He gonna tail him til we can catch up. Don't worry Cel. It ain't over yet!"

Cecilia and Paul, after securing all the evidence and handing it over to the CSI team for analysis, headed back to the office for more questioning with Kendall. He still had 2 hours left on the 48 allowed for holding and Cecilia wanted to get all she could concerning the last case. When they arrived back at the office, Kendall was already waiting for them in one of the interrogation rooms.

"Good morning Mr. Firth. Have you had some time to think about that last case? Do you have anything meaningful to add. I want to assure you that we now have all of the evidence for a charge and probable conviction in Mr. Kunter's case. Now we want to see where we go with you. So are you willing to cooperate in this last thing?" She glanced across the table and was immediately convinced that things were going to come to an end. The look in his eyes suggested desperation and the knowledge they were looking for to wrap things up.

"This last one involves me. It is my fault that this lady is missing a face. Well not exactly but the fact that she is involved is my fault. My sister was concerned about her husband, my brother-in-law. She was convinced he was having an affair. I asked Mr. Stemway to look into it. I told him if he found anything I didn't want him harmed. It would kill my sister and her children to be without a father. Instead, I asked him if there was some way he could fix it so the woman wasn't an issue anymore. It was my belief, based on his previous actions, that he would help me and no one would die because of it. I didn't get any details until it was over and he suggested I tell my sister that the problem was taken care of and she didn't have to worry anymore. I was relieved and in the end, so was she. There really isn't anything else to tell. I never knew the details. I know it was wrong of me to ask. I also know that I was complicit in this particular assault. I just hope you will take into account my cooperation with you and can talk the DA into some type of immunity for me. Do you think that is possible?"

"Well Kendall, I will certainly try. As I said, the DA is always open to negotiations. This is an important case for the city and I am sure she will come to some agreement about your fate. You should know that no matter how it goes down for you, the prosecutor is going to require that you testify as a witness during the trial. That is, if there even is a trial. I would assume he will plead not guilty and this case will continue for the next few months, if not for a year. It will be imperative that you are involved in that part. Do you understand that?" She was confident that an arrangement could be reached for immunity. The fact is that Kendall had no direct influence on any of the victim crimes. He was aware and certainly there was a level of accomplice but his hands-on involvement was non-existent.

"I came to that conclusion yesterday when I agreed to talk. So what next?" He felt like an anvil was lifted off his shoulders. He was obsessed with giving up the information and not being given immunity in exchange. Now that the detective helped alleviate some of that concern, he was confident he was going to be alright. For a quick second, he flashed to an idea that Garrett was released for some reason and hunted him for testifying against him. It was a fleeting second and he realized there was no way he would get bail in these heinous crimes. He was going to jail for a long time.

XXIII

Garrett went straight to his house upon his release. When he opened the back door, he found complete destruction. His entire house was in tatters all around him. Every room was destroyed; there were even holes in the walls as if they were looking for evidence there. He went down to the basement, and discovered there was one cache they did not find. He scraped away the mortar around one of the building blocks and with some effort, removed the false block. Behind it he kept his go bag. It contained everything he would need to escape, if needed. He planned this just as he would have planned an escape route during one of his operations in the jungle.

Inside was enough cash to keep him dark for a few months. There were several changes of clothes and another Glock he had. It also contained a burner phone he picked up at the Walmart. It was a cheap flip phone that he could use to make calls but didn't have any of the smartphone capabilities. He didn't want to add to the odds of being found if he was on the run. He kept the phone off until he needed it and was sure there wasn't any GPS in this particular model. It was the cheapest phone he could find. He went straight upstairs and out to the garage. It was empty except for the scattered debris left from the cabinets he hung along the walls. They had towed his car to the impound lot for evidence.

He left the garage with some urgency and noticed a gold BMW parked on the adjacent corner. There was someone in the driver's seat and he wasn't familiar with this car. He could tell the driver was on the phone and wrote it off to someone that was lost and calling for directions. He headed down the bottom of the hill towards the park and figured he could make his way to the highway. He could make his way to one of the corner bars and call for an Uber. Where to go? All the planning he did for a clean escape and he still hadn't thought about where he would go. *Maybe I should head south to Miami. I can catch a boat from there to the Bahamas. I can call some of my contacts from there and see about IDs and the rest.*

As he headed down the street, he caught a quick glimpse of an Anne Arundel county police car heading up the hill. As he scanned the landscape he noticed another patrol car parked in the lot of the Bingo World at the bottom of the hill. He glanced behind him back up the hill and saw the gold colored BMW, following him down the hill. It was then he realized he was made. They knew who he was and the guy in the BMW must be an undercover officer. He kept walking towards the bottom of the hill, keeping his head about him as always in a stressful situation. When he reached the park, the officers were getting out of their patrol cars. There was an Impala parked on the side of the road and he recognized both of the figures that stepped out. Detectives Young and Dower were walking towards him. He took the backpack off, set it down on the sidewalk in front of him and unzipped the front pocket. Reaching in, he pulled out the Glock....A single shot rang out, scattering the flock of crows that were perched in the oak trees bordering the park; the squawking and fluttering of wings, hundreds of wings at once.

Acknowledgements

This is my first attempt at doing something productive in the last 2 years. I want to give a nod to a few of the people and places that gave me the inspiration to both start and finish this manuscript. In the beginning, there was me and a whole lot of Florida. I came here to finish my Master's degree and wound up in Miami when it was all said and done. I tried, God knows, to get a "real" job. It was post-covid and most of the jobs were flooded with a labor pool that hadn't been witnessed since the Great Depression. I all but gave up on even trying. It was during this time that I decided to start writing outside of the academic world. Anyone that has pursued a post graduate degree can attest to the hours of reading, referencing, and writing. It really isn't the same thing.

I started to read with a voracity that I never thought was inside me. I actually couldn't stand to read when I was younger. My parent's stock answer to boredom was, "Go read a book" or "Go outside". I couldn't be more grateful now for those wonderful suggestions. I spent a large part of my childhood outdoors learning about myself and the wonderful world around me. Now, in my 50's I can't get enough to read. This reading led me to use my expanded vocabulary to express myself through writing. I turns out that I have quite a lot of anecdotes that are easily converted into stories. I started out small: essays, short stories. One day a short story I wrote, "Finlay's Fate" turned into the extended version you have here today.

I spent countless hours in the public library. Specifically, the Coconut Grove Library of Miami-Dade. The staff there have been invaluable, in both my reading and writing needs. I want to give a special thanks to the branch manager, Jennifer Hernandez. Without her uplifting spirit and "can-do" attitude, I would still be staring at an unfinished work. I had some low times and she always seemed to provide the smile and presence I needed to carry on. Without her, I am not sure I would be finished. Christina Fernandez, another librarian there, was invaluable in helping me edit and review my work. I also want to shout out to my creative writing professor in college, John Garot. He provided valuable feedback on this manuscript during my editing phase and value his time and effort in his busy schedule.

After finishing this manuscript, I feel like there is so much more to let out. I am inspired, everyday, by the world around me. Good and Horrible. There is so much in between left untold and undiscovered. I hope to bring the temper to this disparity. Thank you World for giving me what I need to accomplish this task. I hope I can give more as time continues to march on.

S.H. Gochar

www.ingramcontent.com/pod-product-compliance
Lightning Source LLC
Chambersburg PA
CBHW071511140726
47997CB00005B/1934